Read, take home, W9-ASI-138
Donate to Library or to
    Hospital   Rqc 6/24
        or CAST

not Sure that I Read-

Just Like
A Friend

ALSO BY MARILYN SACHS

MARILYN SACHS

Just Like
A Friend

E. P. DUTTON   NEW YORK

Library of Congress Cataloging-in-Publication Data

Sachs, Marilyn.
Just like a friend / Marilyn Sachs.—1st ed.
p. cm.
Summary: Patti finds her relationships with family and
friends changing as she comes to new understandings
about herself, and about her young, lighthearted mother.
ISBN 0-525-44524-2
[1. Parent and child—Fiction.   2. Interpersonal relations—
Fiction.]   I. Title.   89-1168
PZ7.S1187Ju   1989   CIP
[Fic]—dc19   AC

Published in the United States by E. P. Dutton,
a division of Penguin Books USA Inc.

Published simultaneously in Canada by
Fitzhenry & Whiteside Limited, Toronto

Editor: Ann Durell   Designer: Barbara Powderly

Printed in the U.S.A.   First Edition   10 9 8 7 6 5 4 3 2 1 for Bev Gherman

One

Even before the sailor came over to us, Vi had already started giggling.

I acted as if I didn't notice. Either her or him. But I knew what was going to happen. This wasn't the first time.

"Pardon me," the sailor said, looking at Vi as if he didn't really expect her to pardon him, "but does this bus go to Fisherman's Wharf?"

He didn't look much older than me, and I'm only thirteen. His cheeks were nearly as smooth as mine, and round like apples. He was smiling, and as Vi got even more giggly, his mouth curved around into a bigger smile.

"No," I told him. "You're going the wrong way.

You've got to cross the street and take the cable car over there."

He wasn't listening to me at all. Probably he didn't even want to go to Fisherman's Wharf in the first place. He was looking at Vi and trying to get her to look back at him. But she just kept snickering and focusing her eyes down on the ground.

"Where are you girls going anyway?" the sailor asked.

"It's none of your business," I wanted to tell him, but then Vi looked up.

"Home," she told him, really laughing now, so it came out, "Ho-o-me."

The sailor shifted around, pulled at his hat, and flashed her a big grin.

"Well, which way is home?"

"That-a-way," Vi said in her silly voice, pointing up, which made me start laughing, and then all of us were laughing.

"Are you two sisters?" the sailor asked finally.

That really set Vi off, but then our bus came and even though the sailor said something quickly about maybe we could all get together for dinner or maybe . . . there wasn't enough time for him to straighten out all his maybe's before Vi and I were on the bus with our packages, waving good-bye to him as he stood there watching us—really watching Vi—and looking disappointed.

"A nice boy," Vi said. "He really seemed like a nice boy. Maybe we should have invited him home with us."

"Daddy wouldn't have liked it," I told her.

"The last time, when you brought that French student home, Daddy got sore."

That started Vi off again, and it's always hard for me not to join in when Vi gets going like that. So the two of us kind of went crazy. It's very irritating to most grown-ups when that happens, and you could feel people pulling away from us. In front of our seat were two ladies wearing hats. As we got sillier and sillier, you could see their backs stiffen and their hats quiver. Finally, one of them turned around, looked at us—especially at Vi—and said very angrily, "Why don't you just act your age!"

Vi bent down and buried her face in her hands, trying to stifle the sounds of her laughter. But that only made it worse. She sounded like a rhinoceros snorting. I began to get uncomfortable.

"Vi," I said, "Vi—stop it, Vi!"

She finally buried her face in one of the shopping bags we were carrying—the one with the matching pink sweaters we'd just bought at Macy's—and I pretended to look out the window. I always was the first one to feel ashamed.

"Vi was flirting with a sailor," I told Daddy when we got home.

"Rat fink!" Vi said, giving me a quick jab in the ribs with her elbow. Of course, she really wasn't sore. She liked it when I told Daddy.

"Vi!" Daddy said, shaking his head at her.

"Oh, come on, give me a break," Vi told him. "He was just a little lonesome kid. I should have invited him home for dinner."

"Give *me* a break," Daddy said. "The last little

lonesome kid you brought home for dinner stayed for a couple of weeks until I threw him out."

"Don't be a sourpuss," Vi said. Daddy was sitting down in the green club chair with his paper spread out across his legs. Vi just dropped down on his lap, right on top of the newspapers, so hard you could hear him go "Oomph!"

"Are you crazy?" Daddy said. But Vi gave him a big, loud, smacking kiss on top of his bald head, and then he was laughing too. She can always make him laugh.

"Wait till you see what Patti and I bought today," Vi said, jumping up.

"I'm starving," Daddy said. "When are we going to eat?"

"After we try on our new things," Vi said, grabbing the bags. "Come on, Patti, let's give him the special back-to-school fashion show."

"Can't you give it later?" Daddy said. "I'm so hungry, I could even eat tofu."

Vi dragged me along with her toward my room. "Just read your old newspaper," she told him. "Look at the stock pages and figure out how much money you lost today."

Daddy groaned, but we could hear him rustling the paper as we went into my room.

"What should we have for dinner tonight?" I asked her.

"How about steak?" Vi said.

"We still have some leftover lasagna from last night," I told her. "We could have that."

Vi made a face. She was standing in front of

the big mirror over my chest of drawers looking at the face she was making. First it was only her nose wrinkling, but then she raised her upper lip like a rabbit. Then she wrinkled her forehead. Then she crossed her eyes, and finally she just put her face up close to the mirror, turned her head sideways, looked at herself out of the corners of her eyes, and said, "I think I have a rough, red patch right over there, near my left ear. Maybe it's skin cancer. Look over there, Patti, right over there. Tell me if it's a rough, red patch."

I looked. "You must have scratched yourself," I told her. "It's nothing."

She straightened up, still keeping her eyes on her reflection, and moved back a little from the mirror. "I'm really a mess," she said.

She knew she wasn't a mess. She knew she was really gorgeous with her flippy blonde hair, her little nose, her big violet-colored eyes, and her soft rosy skin. There she was, looking at herself in the mirror, and there I was standing right next to her, and looking at her and at me too. We looked alike. I had the same hair color, the same nose, but not the same violet-colored eyes. I had Daddy's brown eyes, his plain brown eyes—which was too bad. Still, I guessed I was kind of pretty, too, even if it was Vi who attracted most of the attention.

"I hate my eyes," I told her. "They're ordinary."

"Let's try on our outfits," she said dreamily, smiling at her face in the mirror. "Just don't tell

Daddy how much the sweaters cost. He'll have a fit."

I told him and he didn't have a fit. He's not that kind of father. He thought Vi's sweater fit her too tightly, but otherwise he liked everything we bought. He usually does.

We had steak for dinner. Vi doesn't like to eat the same thing two nights in a row, even if it is lasagna. We had steak, french fries, salad, french bread, and ice cream with Vi's chocolate mint sauce for dessert.

"I'm getting too fat," Daddy said, after he finished.

"Me too." Vi groaned. "Why did you let me have seconds on the ice cream?"

"Vi can't even fit into size 12 jeans anymore," I told Daddy. "She had to take a 14."

Vi threw a napkin at me.

"The sailor thought she was my sister," I went on. "They never believe she's my mother."

Daddy shook his head at Vi. "She was a size 10 when I first met her," he said, "but otherwise she hasn't changed at all."

Two

I wasn't looking forward to school. My best friend, Jill, had moved away to Philadelphia with her mother and new stepfather. We said we'd write to each other every week. We would never, never stop being best friends. And we did write— for nearly six weeks. She stopped first, but I was getting tired of it too. And anyway, during the summer Vi and I were busy taking tae kwon do, or swimming in Marin, or just generally hanging out.

Except for Jill, Vi was more fun than any kid my own age. But when I entered the schoolyard of my new high school, I felt scared. Jill was gone, and many of the kids I knew from middle school had fanned out to other high schools in the city. Nobody looked familiar, and it seemed as if everybody else had someone to talk to or to laugh with or to look for. I knew all about looking for somebody. For years now I'd come into the schoolyard and looked for Jill. Now there was nobody to look for. But I acted like I was looking for somebody anyway.

I acted like that all through the day, and came home exhausted. Vi was waiting for me.

"Well?" she asked, as soon as I opened the door. "How was school?"

"Rotten," I told her, dropping everything on the floor. "There's nobody in my class that I know, and I sat all by myself during lunch, and I think I want to go to a different high school."

"Poor pussycat," Vi said. She put an arm around my shoulder and led me into the kitchen. There was a plate of assorted cookies on the table—chocolate coconut rolls, pecan shorties, and cherry swirls—all my favorites. The kitchen was fragrant and messy. I knew she'd been baking all day. "I thought we'd have a little party," Vi murmured.

I dropped into a seat and picked up a cherry swirl. "It's scary," I said, "not knowing anybody. Everybody else has a friend except for me. Maybe nobody will like me."

Vi poured both of us glasses of milk and brought them to the table. "Everybody always liked you," she said. "You could have had lots of friends. You just never wanted to be friends with anybody else except Jill." Vi let out a deep sigh. "She's a real great kid, I have to admit. We really had some wonderful times together."

"We sure did," I said, biting into the cookie. "Do you remember the time the three of us went to the planetarium, and Jill dropped an apple under the seat in front of her after the show started and it was all dark? And how when she bent down to pick it up, the lady right in front of her started screaming because she said somebody was feeling her leg, and you couldn't stop laughing . . . ?"

Vi nearly choked over the cookie she was eating, and for a while, the two of us ate cookies, laughed, and reminisced.

"What about that girl Joanie?" Vi asked finally.

"Joanie who?"

"Joanie . . . Joanie . . . I can't remember her last name, but she came for the Christmas party last year. She has red hair . . . a pretty girl with a lot of freckles."

"Oh, Joanie Redding," I said. "Well, I don't know. She's okay, but she's friends with a girl named Sara Russell, and I don't like her. Besides, Joanie didn't even bother to say hi to me today. I saw her in the hall, but she was so busy talking to Sara, she didn't even notice me."

"Well, what about that tall girl—nice, friendly girl. She always gives me a real big hello when I see her. I think her name is Karen."

"No, it's Sharon, Sharon Falls. She is nice, but she went to Lowell."

"Well, I'm not worried," Vi said. "You'll meet somebody nice, and we'll all have fun again just the way we always did with Jill."

She was right—about one part of it, anyway. I did meet somebody nice. The next day, as a matter of fact. Her locker was right next to mine, and it was all so easy. Inside of five minutes, I had made a new best friend.

She was there first, trying to stuff a whole load of things into her locker—not only books and clothes but boxes too. At first, I pretended not to notice, but then a large box fell down and opened up, and pages and pages drifted out, all over the floor. So naturally, I helped her pick everything up, and I couldn't help seeing that there were poems on all the pages and that some of the words in the poems couldn't possibly have been part of a school assignment.

I must have looked surprised, because she said quickly as she took the papers back from me, "They're my poems. I wrote them."

I said, "Oh!"

You wouldn't think she'd be interested in somebody who just said, "Oh!" after she'd said she was a poet. But then I noticed that one of the pages had drifted over to the middle of the hall and that a boy was just about to step on it, and I screamed out "Stop!" and rushed over and picked it up just as his foot was coming down on it.

After that, it all fell right into place.

Her name was Emily Rees; she was not in my homeroom, but she was a ninth grader too; she lived six blocks away from me; she had two older brothers, parents she couldn't stand, wore contact lenses, had no best friend, and asked me to meet her down in the lunchroom at noon over near the door to the schoolyard.

"I don't want *her* to see them," she said while we were eating lunch together. "That's why I decided I'd better just keep them in my locker to be on the safe side. I wrote a lot this summer. *She'd* tear the place apart if she ever found out everything I wrote."

She was Emily's mother.

"I can show my mother anything," I told her.

"You're lucky," she said. "My mother is the biggest prude that ever lived. My father too. They're both dinosaurs."

"My mother was pregnant before she married my father," I said. "Maybe that's why she's so understanding. Besides, she's not even thirty-two yet. Our birthdays are exactly six months apart. I'll be fourteen on November twelfth, and she'll be thirty-two on May twelfth. Isn't it strange that both of us were born on the same day?"

"My mother is older than my father," Emily said. "Six years older. She was married once before she married my father, and she had Jeff. Then she married my father, and they had Tim. I know I was an accident. God, they're practically old enough to be my grandparents. My father is forty-six and my mother is fifty-two."

"That is pretty old," I agreed. "My father is fifty-one. My grandmother is fifty-three, and she says he's old enough to be my mother's father. She doesn't like my father very much. She was really angry when my mother got pregnant, and she gave them both a hard time before she let them get married."

"Everybody's old in my family. Jeff is eleven years older than me, and Tim is seven. Neither of them lives at home anymore, but whenever they're home, they're just as bad as my parents. They all pick on me and act like I'm some kind of freak."

"My father's not so bad," I said cautiously. I knew that both of my parents were great and that I was very lucky compared to most kids. So I always tried to sound a little cool whenever I spoke about them. "He's pretty old, but he doesn't really hassle me."

"My father's a real jellyfish," Emily said. "He only gets into the act when she makes him. But naturally, he always backs her even when she's wrong, which she generally is." She looked inside her sandwich and made a face. "All I could find in the house this morning to make a sandwich out of was some stale rye bread and some dry peanut butter. Yuck! I can't eat this stuff." Emily crushed the rest of her sandwich and stuffed it back into the bag. Then she looked over at me and my sandwich. "What are you eating?" she asked.

"Oh, it's just—walnut cream cheese on raisin bread." I didn't tell her that Vi had fixed it for me, that she fixed my lunch every day. "Do you want a piece?"

"Sure. It can't be any worse than mine."

I handed her the other half of my sandwich and watched her snap off a piece and chew it. I liked her face—a thin, dark, angry face with big, dark, angry eyes. And I liked the way she talked, too. She wasn't anything like Jill, who was small, chunky, smiley, and kind of sleepy looking.

"Whatever I do is wrong," Emily said. "If I'm out with my friends, she says how come I don't stay home more. If I'm home reading, she says how come I don't go out more. And this summer, when I really got into writing my poems, she didn't stop." Emily screwed up her face and began talking high up in her nose. " 'It's not normal for a girl your age to sit around a whole summer writing poems. Go out and have some fun.' 'I am having fun,' I told her, 'or I would be having fun, if you would just leave me alone.' And then she kept asking me to show her my poems. She's dying to see my poems."

"Oh, no!" I said, remembering some of the words I'd noticed in the poems.

Emily swallowed the last bite of my sandwich. "This isn't bad," she said. "Do you have another one?"

"No," I said, "but my mother baked some cookies yesterday." I showed her the cookies Vi had packed in my lunch, and she selected a cherry swirl and a pecan shortie.

"Why did you say 'Oh, no'?" she asked, and took a bite out of a cookie.

"I don't know," I said nervously.

"This is good." Emily swallowed the rest of the cookie, and smiled and nodded at me. "You're the first person I've met in ages that I could get an intelligent word out of."

"No kidding!" I could feel an idiot smile spreading over my face.

"Except for Cameron." Emily lowered her face a little, raised her eyebrows, and gave me a deep, deep look.

"Who's Cameron?" I asked.

"He's a guy." Emily put her head back and laughed. Her neck was thin, and something bulged in the middle of her throat in an exciting way.

"What class is he in?" I asked.

"Oh, he doesn't go to this school." Emily shook her head slowly, and narrowed her eyes. "He's sixteen and a half, and he goes to Lowell."

"Oh!" I said.

"Some of my poems are about him." She leaned forward across the table, and I leaned forward too.

"Does your mother know about him?" I whispered.

"He lives upstairs in my building," Emily murmured, "but she doesn't really know anything. Anything important."

"Oh!" Why did I have to keep saying "Oh"?

"Except . . . she found one of my poems before school started. She must have been sneaking around. That's why I'm going to be keeping them in my locker from now on. She's always snooping around. Is your mother like that?"

"Well, no, but . . ."

"So she found it." Emily jerked her body upwards. "It was like a bomb hit the place."

"Well, what did she say?"

Emily rolled her eyes around and shook her head back and forth. "I never saw her so mad in my whole life." Emily began laughing. "She said she didn't think she'd ever get over the kind of things I said about her in the poem. She said she never knew I felt that way about her, and she began crying and crying—it was disgusting. But I just kept telling her that if you keep snooping around, you're going to find things you're not going to want to see, and that it served her right for poking her nose where it didn't belong."

"But wasn't the poem about Cameron?"

"No, no, it was all about her. About how I felt about her. It was called 'My Mother, My Enemy.' If you want to see it, I'll fish it out of my locker and show it to you."

"Well, sure I'd like to see it. But then what happened?"

"What happened when?"

"Afterwards. After your mother read the poem. What happened afterwards?"

"Well, there's not going to be any afterwards. I'm going to be more careful and keep them here in school. But I'll show them to you if you want to see them. I'll even show you some of my poems about Cameron."

"Oh, thanks, Emily. I'd like to see them."

"Not all of them," Emily said. "Of course, I

couldn't show you all of them. But I will show you the tamer ones."

She was smiling at me, and I smiled back. I couldn't wait to bring her home and introduce her to Vi.

Three

"Isn't that terrible!" Vi said when I told her about Emily and her mother. "You wouldn't believe in this day and age that a modern mother could be so . . . so . . ." Vi couldn't even think of a word to describe Emily's mother, so she waved both hands around, making floppy circles in the air.

"So that's why she has to hide all her poems in her locker at school."

Vi shook her head. "You'd think she'd just be bursting with pride to have a kid who wrote poems. If it was me, I'd just think it was absolutely marvelous, and I'd be so proud. . . ."

I didn't say anything.

Vi looked at me and reached over quickly to take my hand. "Not that I'm not proud of you,

Patti. You know that. I think you're the greatest. But I mean if I had another kid who wrote poetry. I wasn't talking about you, Patti. I love you just the way you are."

Crazy to be suddenly jealous of Emily just because Vi seemed so impressed. Even crazier to be jealous of that other sister of mine who wrote poetry, and would never be born. Not that Vi didn't want more kids. But Daddy said no. "Two girls are enough," he always said. He meant Vi when he said two girls—Vi and me. She always told me how much she wanted more kids, and still did, but he didn't.

I was happy I didn't have sisters or brothers because I wanted Vi all to myself. I didn't want her to love anybody else the way she loved me. Daddy didn't count. Vi loved him too, and that was fine. She could love him and me. Nobody else.

"She's got a boyfriend named Cameron," I said slowly. "He goes to Lowell, and he's sixteen and a half."

"When are you bringing her home?" Vi asked, her eyes shining. "I'm dying to meet her."

Emily couldn't come the next day. She had a piano lesson after school. We did eat our lunch together, and she showed me two poems she'd written the night before. One was about Cameron.

CAMERON
Arms, legs, mouths, teeth
Tongues, fingers, toes
Breasts, hips, backs

Elbows, knees, throats
Where do you end
And I begin?

I could feel the heat rising to the roots of my hair. I wanted to ask her what it all meant, what she and Cameron were doing, but I didn't even know how to frame the question.

"Well?" she asked, taking another bite out of the half of the pesto, cheese, and tomato sandwich I'd given her.

"Uh . . ." I said, ". . . uh . . . Is it . . . I mean . . . Did . . . uh . . . Cameron . . . ?"

"No," she said, "he hasn't seen it yet. Maybe I'll save it and give him a whole bunch of them for Christmas. Maybe I'll bind them in a special binding or even buy one of those beautiful iridescent silk-covered books they sell down on Union Street and fill it with my poems. I could call it *The Book of Cameron* or maybe *Cameron's Book.* What do you think?"

"Well, sure," I said. "Sure."

"No, I mean, should I call it *The Book of Cameron* or *Cameron's Book*?"

"Oh, well, I don't know."

Emily nodded, finished the sandwich half, and reached over to take one of the jelly-filled strawberry cupcakes Vi had put into my lunch bag. "You haven't seen the others yet," she said. "Maybe you'll be able to make up your mind after you've looked at the others. Of course, I can't show you all of them." She gave a quick little laugh and then held out another paper. "Here, see what you think of this one."

> *TO* _____
> *The shadows on your face*
> *In the darkened hall*
> *The thundering footsteps of the others*
> *Racing by*
> *And then our eyes meet*
> *And we smile*
> *And know*
> *That it was meant to be*
> *And something had begun.*

At first, I didn't understand. "Is this about Cameron?" I asked. "About how you met him?"

"Are you crazy?" Emily said, offering me a piece of my orange. "Read it again. It has nothing to do with Cameron."

I read it again, and felt the tears rising in my eyes. It was about me. About how we had met yesterday. About how she felt about our friendship. I couldn't speak at first.

"Well?" she said, looking into my empty lunch bag. "Well?"

"It's about me," I whispered.

Emily put down the bag and smiled. "Yes, it is," she said.

"Nobody ever wrote a poem about me," I told her, trying not to cry.

"Oh, it won't be the last," Emily said, reaching over and patting my hand. "I'm writing all the time now. Even when I'm not writing, I'm writing. Lately, I think poems whatever I'm doing. Even now in this smelly lunchroom, I'm thinking poems. I'm thinking, 'Down in the grayness of this unfriendly place . . .' I think that would be a great beginning for a poem. Or maybe an end. But all the time, lines keep popping into my head."

"I think it's wonderful," I said.

"So do I," Emily said.

"I never think poems," I told her. "I don't know what I think."

"Don't you ever think about boys?"

"Well, sure," I said. "I think about boys a lot."

Then both of us were laughing, and Emily leaned forward. "Like who?" she asked.

I told her. "There's this boy in my class, Dan Green, in my homeroom class. He was in my class last term too, and I've known him since fourth grade. But since last year, I've been noticing things about him—like his arms. He has veins that show on his arms. I don't exactly know why, but I like the way his arms look. I told Vi, and she said . . ."

"Who's Vi?" Emily looked upset.

"Vi? She's my mother."

"Your mother?" Emily said, surprised. "You call your mother Vi?"

"Yes," I said. "That's her name. Violet. But everybody calls her Vi."

"I could never call my mother by her first name," Emily said. "She'd kill me if I did, and besides, I wouldn't want to anyway."

"Well, Vi likes it," I told her. "And she's not

like other mothers. She's more like a friend than a mother."

Emily's eyebrows rose.

"You'll see," I said. "Wait until you meet her. Everybody likes Vi."

Emily came home with me the next day, and Vi was waiting for us. Naturally, the kitchen was a mess, but there were two kinds of brownies sitting on the kitchen table—butterscotch marshmallow and chocolate fudge. Vi had set out red, white, and blue glasses on a red paper tablecloth with little blue paper napkins that showed firecrackers exploding on them. I think they were left over from our Fourth of July celebration.

"What's happening?" Emily said when she saw the table.

"You're happening," Vi said, giggling. "We're just so pleased you're here."

"Oh!" Emily said. I began laughing too—Vi and I were both laughing, while Emily stood there, looking at the table. Any minute now I expected she would look up and start laughing too. But she didn't.

"It's nice to meet you, Mrs. Carmichael," Emily mumbled finally.

"Oh, don't call me that." Vi made a face. "None of the kids call me that. Call me Vi. But sit down, Emmy, sit down."

Emily sat down.

Vi stood up, looking at her and grinning. "Do you know who she looks like, Patti? She looks like that girl on the Romeo spaghetti commercial."

"Which girl?"

"Not the big blonde one cooking. The little dark, thin one who's dancing. You know—you see her spinning around in her little leotard and then coming home and eating that big plate of spaghetti."

I studied Emily. She had an angry look on her face which surprised me. Not that Emily didn't usually have an angry look on her face, but Vi had just compared her to a dancer on TV. You'd think that would have made her happy. And she was quiet, too, which was surprising. I guessed she was more shy than I had realized. But I knew that if there was anybody who could make her relax, it would be Vi.

"Maybe," I said. "But I think Emily's even thinner than the girl on TV. What do you think, Emily?"

"Uh—what?" Emily said in a cranky voice.

"Do you think you look anything like the girl on the Romeo spaghetti commercial?"

"The what?"

"The Romeo spaghetti commercial. It comes on just before 'Dynasty,'" Vi explained.

"I never saw it," Emily said. "I don't watch much TV."

Vi filled the glasses with milk and sat down. She offered the plate with the chocolate brownies to Emily. "No thanks," Emily said. Vi offered her the plate with the butterscotch marshmallow brownies. "No thanks," Emily said.

"It's all right," Vi told her. "You can take one.

You're so thin you don't have to worry about your figure. And besides, there aren't any calories in these brownies." Vi began laughing.

Emily took one of the brownies, and put it down on her blue napkin. "Thank you, Mrs. Carmichael," she said.

"Call me Vi," Vi told her.

Vi and I ate a bunch of brownies, but Emily left hers sitting on her plate. "Lunchtime," I told Vi, "she eats like a horse."

"A pony, maybe," Vi said, and the two of us laughed. But not Emily.

"Where's your room?" she said finally, to me.

Vi jumped up. "Come on, Emmy," she said. "I'll show you where it is."

But first she showed Emily the living room, Daddy's study, and then the two bathrooms. "I couldn't believe it when we moved into this condo," she said. "Only two bedrooms, not counting the study, but two great big, full bathrooms. And just look at the tub in this one. It's for the master bedroom. Just look. It has a Jacuzzi in it. That's the way it came. I just couldn't believe this place. At home, we had three bedrooms and one lousy little bathroom. Every morning, there'd be a real knock-down, drag-out brawl to get into it. I remember one morning, my brother actually broke the lock on the door trying to get in. I was inside. Anyway, my mother just about hit the ceiling."

"Tell her about the time he locked himself inside and you climbed along the ledge and came in through the window," I said.

"We have two and a half bathrooms in my house," Emily said, looking at me. "Where's your room, Patti?"

"Oh, it's over here," Vi said. "But first, you have to see this big dressing room in my bedroom. Here, you have to look out the window to see that gorgeous view. No, you're not looking the right way, Emmy. Over there. Isn't it gorgeous?"

"Sure—yes—sure—it's great," said Emily.

Just then the phone rang. When Vi went off to answer it, Emily said, "Can't we go somewhere by ourselves?"

"By ourselves?"

"I mean without your mother. Where we can talk."

"We can talk in front of my mother. She's really been looking forward to meeting you."

We went into my room and sat down on my bed, but we could hear Vi laughing as she talked on the phone to somebody—probably Daddy. He usually called her once or twice a day. Emily got up, walked over to the door, and closed it.

"Now we can talk," she said.

Four

Everything was different in Emily's house. To begin with, her mother wasn't home when we arrived.

"She's a psychologist," Emily said. "Her office is actually right in this building so she can sneak in and spy on me any time she likes."

"I'd like to meet her," I said.

"Why?" Emily took my arm and led me through a living room with a large red and blue Persian rug on the floor and gray sectional pieces of furniture arranged stiffly around it. The room was neat and orderly, with a few large paintings on the wall. Our own living room was crammed with the pieces of furniture that Vi kept buying, and all the walls in our apartment were covered with posters, photos, paintings, and wall hangings. Daddy said that our place was beginning to look like a junkyard and told Vi to stop putting things up on the walls. Sometimes she would take an old poster or painting down to make room for a new one, but most of the time she'd find a space even if it was tiny or high up on the wall.

Emily's kitchen was white and black and very neat. No dishes in the sink or flour on the floor. Emily opened the refrigerator. "Nothing, as usual," she said. "You'd think she'd remember we were out of milk. I told her last night and again this morning but, no, she's just too busy to think of me."

"Why don't we go down and pick up some milk?" I suggested.

"I don't want to go down," Emily said sulkily. "She should have remembered. I told her. I bet you don't have to tell your mother."

I didn't answer and tried to look enthusiastic when Emily pulled out a bottle of tomato juice from the refrigerator. I'm really not crazy about tomato juice.

"Of course she didn't remember to pick up any cookies, either," Emily said, opening a cabinet door and looking inside.

"Oh, that's okay," I said quickly. "I don't want any cookies anyway."

Emily found a can of salted Spanish nuts, so we ended up eating them and drinking some of the tomato juice. Then we went to Emily's room.

"Wow!" I said, because as neat and orderly as the rest of the house was, Emily's room looked as if it had been tossed around on a tidal wave. The bed was unmade and rumpled. Clothes were strewn all over the tops of the chairs and furniture and even on the floor. A trash can was overflowing with papers, and it didn't seem as if there was any clear place one could sit down.

Emily looked around her with satisfaction. "She doesn't like it," Emily said. "But I tell her, you can do whatever you like with the rest of the place, but my room is my room and I can do whatever I like in my room."

"And she doesn't clean it up?"

"She'd better not," Emily said. She pushed some clothes and books off a chair and motioned for me to sit down. I eased myself down carefully and watched Emily flop onto her bed, over the twisted pile of sheets, blankets, and clothes. I thought of my own room, a little crowded and messy maybe, but comfortable and pretty. And I thought how Vi always kept it clean and cozy for me.

"I like it this way," Emily said. "The rest of this place looks like a morgue."

That got us laughing, and pretending we were corpses. Emily tied a stocking around her neck as if she'd been strangled, stuck out her tongue, rolled her eyes up in her head, and flopped back on her bed with her arms outstretched. I made believe I had been a victim of a heart attack from seeing a ghost. We went through a variety of different deaths, mostly violent, and I was just hanging over Emily's desk, with my hair streaming down and a make-believe knife in my back when Emily's mother walked into the room.

"Oh," Emily said. "I didn't hear you come in."

Emily's mother looked like Emily—small, dark, and thin. But unlike Emily she had a wide smile on her face. "It looks like a good time is being had by all."

I straightened myself out and stood up.

"This must be Patti," said Emily's mother. "We've been hearing a lot about you these past few days."

"There's no milk," Emily said.

"Hi, Mrs. Rees," I mumbled. "I'm glad to meet you."

"And I'm glad to meet you too, Patti," Mrs. Rees said pleasantly. "And I didn't mean to interrupt you. It looked as if you were having a really deep philosophical discussion when I came in."

I laughed, but Emily said, "And there's no cookies either."

"Well, why didn't you pick some up?" Mrs. Rees cocked her head to one side and inspected me. "My, you certainly are a pretty girl," she said. I decided I liked Emily's mother. "How tall are you?"

"I'm five-eight."

Mrs. Rees nodded and turned, still smiling, to Emily. "How was school today?"

Emily scowled. "Boring as usual. The same as it is every day."

" 'The song of canaries,' " said her mother. "Well, I just looked in to say hello. I've got to run."

"I guess one of your precious patients is waiting for you," Emily said.

"You've got it," said her mother, turning towards me again. "Nice meeting you, Patti. Come often."

"There's nothing in the house for dinner," Emily said as her mother moved out of the room.

"I know," Mrs. Rees said. "We'll go out for dinner."

"Where?" Emily shouted, leaning out the door of the room.

"Wherever you like," came her mother's voice, "except for Mexican."

"I like Mexican," Emily yelled.

When she came back into the room, I asked her, "What did your mother mean when she said, 'The song of canaries?' "

"Oh!" Emily waved one hand around. "It's a poem—'The song of canaries / Never varies.' "

"What does that mean?"

"It means," Emily said crankily, "that she thinks I'm always complaining."

"Well, you are," I said, laughing. "I agree with your mother."

Emily threw a pillow at me, and I threw it back. We tossed around a few other things, but it didn't make any difference to the appearance of the room.

Emily came down with me in the elevator. As we were getting out, a short, thin boy with glasses got in. Emily squeezed my arm. "Hi, Cameron," she said.

The boy looked at her for a moment, and then said, "Oh—hi," just before the doors closed.

"Well?" Emily asked me. "Well, what did you think of him?"

"Was that Cameron?"

"Of course it was Cameron. Didn't you hear me say, 'Hi, Cameron'?"

"Yes, I did, but I really didn't have a chance to get a good look at him."

"Did you see the jacket he was wearing?" Emily said dreamily. "I love that jacket. It's my favorite jacket. It's the same color as his eyes. Did you notice his eyes?"

"No, I didn't have much of a chance to notice anything except that he's short and wears glasses."

"His hair is curly," Emily said. "I wrote a whole poem just about his hair. I'll say it for you because it's a short one." We walked out of her building, and Emily said:

> "Cameron's hair curls and ripples
> In my hand
> Cameron's hair weaves a net of love
> Around my fingers."

I waited for more, but she had stopped.

"Is that all?" I asked her.

"It's a short poem," she said. "Did you like it?"

"I don't know much about poetry," I explained. "But I don't think I understand it."

Her face was close to mine, and I could smell the salted Spanish peanuts on her breath.

"Come on," she said, linking an arm with mine. "I'll walk you home. What don't you understand?"

I was happy being with her, happy having her for my friend. I really liked her. She wasn't easy to understand the way Jill was, but she was exciting. I was also feeling less and less awkward and embarrassed with her, more and more myself, more confident. I couldn't figure her out yet. There were some things about her that didn't fit. It was like a puzzle that I would eventually solve. I wasn't in a hurry. I was enjoying myself too much.

"Well, I don't think I understand what you're saying in the poem. I mean, are you saying that you're actually holding Cameron's hair in your hand, or . . ."

"Yes," Emily said softly. "That's what I'm saying."

"So that means that you and Cameron . . ."

Emily laughed a hoarse little laugh and squeezed my arm meaningfully.

"But he hardly said anything to you in the elevator. He didn't even seem to know who you were."

"Boy, are you inexperienced!" Emily said.

I nodded respectfully. "Yes," I said, "I am. Not like you."

"Oh, well!" Emily gave me a kindly pat on the back. "Maybe you're just a late bloomer."

"Is Cameron your first boyfriend?"

"Of course not," Emily said. "Watch out for that car." She gripped my arm and hurried me across the street. I couldn't wait to get to the other side and continue the conversation. Boys were beginning to occupy more and more of my thoughts. Vi always said it was perfectly natural to think about boys, and that I should remember that they were probably thinking about me. Grandma said I should not think about boys but should concentrate on school. Jill and I had talked about all the different boys we both knew, and speculated on which ones liked us. But Jill was inexperienced too. I had a feeling that the conversations Emily and I were going to have would be different and much, much more exciting.

"You mean to say you've never gone out with a single boy in your whole life?" Emily asked when we crossed the street.

"No," I admitted. "Except last year at the Halloween party, we had boys as well as girls for the first time, and this kid, Noah Bernstein, pushed my head down when we were ducking for apples and chased me around the living room later, and then, in school, he and I worked on a science project together and went to the museum. Then, during the school picnic last spring, he said we should go to a ball game during the summer, but we never did. Besides, I really like Dan Green better. I wish I'd asked him to the Halloween party last year. Maybe I will this year."

"What Halloween party is that?" Emily asked.

"At my house. We've always had a Halloween party ever since I can remember. Vi and I spend a whole week carving out millions of pumpkins to decorate the place with. And the night of the party, we put out all the lights and just have candles in the pumpkins, and spiders hanging from the ceilings, and skeletons in all the closets. And we have orange punch and lots of cookies. And we play games—you'll see. You'll be coming this year."

"And both your parents are there too?"

I laughed out loud. "Are you kidding? My father wouldn't be caught dead at one of our parties. We can't even get him to help carve the pumpkins. He generally goes out for the evening."

"But your mother?"

"Oh, sure! She always has as much fun as the rest of us. Anyway, I've never really gone out with a boy. When did you start?"

Emily waved her hand impatiently. "I can't remember."

"Well, how old were you?"

"Mmm. Maybe eleven and a half. Maybe twelve."

"What was his name?"

"I'm not sure."

"You're not sure what his name was?"

"No. I mean I'm not sure which one I dated first. Maybe Roger. Maybe Michael." Emily shrugged. "They didn't mean anything to me. Not the way Cameron does. I never even wrote any poems about them."

"Well, tell me about Cameron. Tell me how you met him and how you started dating. Tell me how you got him to notice you. I'd like to learn how to get Dan Green to notice me."

"Maybe he notices you already."

"No. I don't think he does. I mean he'll say hi and talk to me if I ask him something about school. But I don't think he notices me. I guess I'll just ask him to the party. You can invite Cameron too if you like."

Emily snorted. "Cameron wouldn't come to a kid's party," she said. "Come on, Patti. He's six-teen and a half. He's not going to come to a party where everybody is thirteen or fourteen, and where your mother is around."

Cameron didn't come to the Halloween party. Emily did. And so did Dan Green. I asked him along with a whole bunch of other kids, new kids mostly, I'd been meeting. For some reason, it was getting easier for me to make friends. There was Felissa Roth, my partner in P.E., tall, dark-eyed, and with a way of tossing her long, dark hair out of her eyes that I tried to copy even though I never had any hair in my own eyes. There was Joey Lee, on the track team, and Ryan Kingman, who was so funny you started laughing before he even said anything. He did magic tricks that mostly didn't work, and that was funny too.

Suddenly I had a lot of friends, and I invited them all to my party. I think most of them had a really good time. I know I did. Dan Green kept tickling the back of my neck with one of the spi-ders he pulled down from the ceiling, and he stayed after the party to help Vi and me clean up. Vi said she thought he was a real nice boy with a great sense of humor.

The only bad thing was that Emily left early. She said the party was just too babyish for her.

Five

Emily was smart. Everybody said so. "She's real smart," Vi said. "Maybe that's why she always looks so grumpy." "That girl certainly has a head on her shoulders," Daddy said. "She's too smart for her own good," said my grandma. "It runs in the family," Mrs. Rees explained. "My brother is brilliant, and so is my son Jeff. Emily may not be brilliant, but she can certainly hold her own."

But for such a smart girl, in some ways she really was stupid.

"How come you always leave your poems lying all over your room if you don't want your mother to see them?"

I'd been noticing each time I visited Emily that

her poems were generally strewn everywhere in her room. And not buried under the usual piles of papers, clothing, and assorted junk either. Usually, the poems lay right on top. Generally, they were the most explicit poems about Cameron or the most hateful ones about her mother.

"It would serve her right if she saw them," Emily said. "She's not supposed to come snooping around in my room, and she knows it."

"But I thought you don't *want* her to see the poems."

"Of course I don't. Not that she's interested anyway."

"But I thought you said she was interested. That you had to keep everything in your locker at school so that she wouldn't find out what you were writing and get upset. But some of these poems are copies of the ones you have at school."

"You just don't understand," Emily said.

It was true. There was a lot I didn't understand about Emily and her mother.

One evening, when her father was out of town, Emily invited me to go out to dinner with her and her mother.

"She said you could pick the place," Emily said. "Where would you like to go?"

"How about a Chinese restaurant?"

Emily made a face. "We just went to a Chinese restaurant the other day."

"Well, how about an Italian restaurant? I like Figaro's."

"I'm sick of Italian food," Emily said, "but if you really want to go . . ."

"No, no. We can go somewhere else. I know your mother doesn't like Mexican."

"Who told you that? She likes Mexican. And if you want to go to a Mexican restaurant, that's okay. She said you could pick the place."

"I thought she said she didn't like Mexican food."

"Look, Patti, do you like Mexican food?"

"Sure I do, but I like other . . ."

"Great! We'll go to a Mexican restaurant. How about El Sombrero? They have the greatest hot tamales. I love hot tamales."

"Well, if you're sure your mother wouldn't mind."

"You're the one who's picking," said Emily.

Mrs. Rees didn't comment on how she felt about Mexican food, but she ordered a salad that night. She seemed in good spirits, though, as she usually did. Emily also seemed in good spirits, wolfing down her hot tamale and saying ecstatically how delicious it was. And I was in good spirits, too. Mrs. Rees kept asking me questions about myself, and I love it when people ask me questions about myself.

"Do you read a lot, Patti?"

"Not as much as Emily. Vi says—Vi is my mother—that I should read more and watch less TV. She says the two of us should read more and watch less TV."

"It's not so bad watching a certain amount of TV," said Mrs. Rees. "It keeps you in touch with other people."

Emily looked up from her tamale. "Come on,

Mother, get off it. You know what you think of people who watch TV. You call them frozen couch potatoes."

Emily's mother laughed. She had the same bulge in her throat as Emily, and the same exciting way of throwing her head back. "Emily doesn't let me get away with anything," she said. "But I'm talking about occasional TV watching, not addictive. It's okay to watch a ball game or a program that other people watch. It's okay to be a part of your own generation. It wouldn't hurt Emily to watch a little TV now and then."

Emily stopped chewing her piece of tamale. She had another piece raised on her fork, but she lowered it and looked at her mother out of a tight, grim face. "And what is that supposed to mean?"

Emily's mother put a piece of lettuce into her mouth, chewed thoughtfully, swallowed, and said in a kindly, comforting voice, "This is no criticism of you, dear. I think you're fine just the way you are. But you are a bit of a snob, you know. And I do think a little TV, not much but enough to be aware of what other people are enjoying, can be a bridge."

Emily laid down her fork. "I didn't need a bridge to make friends with Patti."

"No, that's true," said Mrs. Rees, smiling. Then, changing the subject, she asked me what subject I enjoyed most in school.

"Math," I told her. "I love math. I love the way there's only one right answer. I don't like subjects like English, where different people can have different ideas and everybody is right."

"I have a lot of friends who watch TV," Emily said.

"I know you do, dear. Don't fixate."

"You started it," Emily said. "You were the one who said I was a snob."

"Yes, I did." Mrs. Rees buttered a small piece of a tortilla and took a little bite. "But it's not such a terrible thing being a snob. We're all snobs in our family. And I guess you wouldn't be writing poetry if you weren't a snob." She turned to me. "Has Emily showed you any of her poems?"

"Uh—well—yes," I mumbled.

"Silly question." Mrs. Rees took another bite of her tortilla. "Emily shows her poems to anybody who's even faintly interested. And they certainly are remarkable."

Emily stood up and shouted, "I hate you! I hate you!" and rushed off to the rest room.

"Now what did I say?" said Mrs. Rees, looking puzzled.

"She always cuts me down," Emily said later, when we were sitting in her room. Her face was stiff with anger.

"But Emily, she really doesn't seem to mind your poems. I think she's even proud of them. She said they were remarkable. Maybe because she's a psychologist, she hears a lot of pretty strong stuff, so she doesn't get shocked easily. Maybe you just don't understand her."

"She doesn't understand me," Emily said, and began crying.

I didn't understand her either, but I put an arm around her and tried to comfort her. More and more I was beginning to wonder about some of the things Emily said had happened and what actually had happened.

"Take Cameron, for instance," I said one day to Vi. "She always acts like he's her boyfriend, but whenever we meet him in the elevator or on the street, it seems as if he hardly knows who she is."

Vi and I were standing in front of the mirror, looking at ourselves. I had on a new shirt that we had just bought for me to wear to my birthday party in November. My fourteenth. It was a dark red one with a bright pink silky sash. I liked the way I looked, and so did Vi. Both of us were looking at me this time in the mirror.

"You're really a knockout, Patti. Do you know that?" Vi reached over and straightened one side of the sash without taking her eyes off my mirror image.

"Do you really like it, Vi? You don't think it makes me look too fat?"

"Fat?" Vi said, shaking her head. "You've been getting skinny on me. Just look at the two of us. I look like a fat blimp next to you."

Of course she didn't look like a blimp. She looked as lovely as ever, but I'd been growing and was now about half a head taller than she, and slimmer.

"You've really got a very nice figure," Vi said. "I'm kind of lumpy all around, and just look at my hips. But you've got a nice little waist, and not too much up or down."

"Grandma says I take after her. She says you

take after the women on your father's side of the family. They all had big busts and big butts. But she says she was always tall and slim."

"Like a stick." Vi giggled and put an arm around my waist. I put an arm around her shoulders, and we leaned our heads together.

When I was little, I always believed that I would grow up to look exactly like Vi even though our eyes weren't the same color. I think I believed, or wanted to believe, that my eyes might change and become violet just like hers. Later on, I worried that I might not look exactly like her, and sometimes I even cried. But now here I was, looking at myself in the mirror, at me, with my brown eyes, and my tall, slim figure, and my face that was something like Vi's and yet completely different, and I wasn't upset at all. I liked what I saw in the mirror.

"Emily's small all around. She's a size 5, but she eats more than I do. Generally, she eats half my lunch as well as hers."

"I'd better put in an extra sandwich from now on," Vi said. "Maybe that's why you're getting so thin."

"No, don't," I told her. "I like me this way."

After my birthday party in November, some of the kids who came—Felissa Roth, Joanie Redding, Ryan Kingman, Joey Lee, and, naturally, Dan Green—began eating lunch together in the lunchroom. They wanted me and Emily to join them. Emily said no. She said we should keep on eating lunch just by ourselves. She said the kids, except for Dan, were all immature, and the girls all show-offs. She said she would understand, though, if I preferred their company to hers.

Of course I ate lunch with her, and read some of her new poems about Cameron. Emily and I were best friends, and she seemed to want me all to herself. I used to be that way with Jill, so I understood how she felt. But I had changed. Now it was exciting for me watching other people's faces turn up in smiles when they saw me coming down the hall, or having somebody call after me to wait up in the yard, or just talking and laughing with kids who wanted to be with me. I liked it, but I didn't want to upset Emily, so the two of us stayed by ourselves in the lunchroom for a while. Gradually the other kids began moving closer and closer to where we sat. And one day, when I got down to the lunchroom a few minutes late, Ryan Kingman was sitting next to Emily, trying out one of his magic tricks on her—one with a disappearing coin that kept appearing and falling out of his sleeve.

"You've just got it all wrong," Emily was saying. But she was laughing too, and when Ryan said he was going to make her disappear, and flapped a white scarf over her head, she began laughing so hard she couldn't stop.

After that, we all ate lunch together, and Emily stopped writing poems about Cameron.

Six

Vi loved to dance. Disco, rock and roll, ballroom, even square dancing—once the music started, Vi would be up on her feet, ready to go.

Sometimes, she'd even be able to coax Daddy to dance with her, especially for the slower dances. His firm gave a formal dinner dance once a year, in February, and Vi always came back bubbling over with pleasure about the marvelous evening she'd spent and all the great partners she'd danced with. Generally, Daddy went right to bed, but Vi would come and sit on my bed and wake me up if I'd been asleep and tell me everything.

Ever since I'd been a little girl, those nights

were like bright candles of memory in my mind. One year, Vi wore a strapless red satin dress that kept slipping while she danced. Another year, she sprained her ankle so badly spinning around that she had to wear an ace bandage for weeks, and use a cane.

For each dinner dance Vi bought a new dress. Daddy always argued with her, complaining that it was foolish to spend a fortune just for one night and telling her to wear the dress from last year. But when it was time to leave and she came whirling into the room wearing the new dress, her hair set, her face made up, her eyes shining, and her feet already tapping, ready for the dance, he would just shake his head, smile, and maybe reach out and give her a kiss. He was so proud of her, and even though he complained about all the money she spent, he liked showing her off to his friends. None of them, he always said, had a wife who could hold a candle to her. He meant in looks.

This year, Vi's dress was an off-the-shoulders, deep peach-colored satin with a slit skirt trimmed with rhinestones. She wore rhinestones in her hair, had rhinestones trimming her silver sandals, and when she twirled around, the lights twinkled in her hair and on her feet.

"The band's going to be The King Leers," she cried. "Do you remember them, Patti? No, of course you wouldn't, but they were real big in the sixties and seventies. Oh, they are one wild group, and I guess we'll be able to dance all those great rock and roll dances like the boogaloo and the monkey. This is going to be the best dinner dance yet."

"You say that every year, Vi," I told her. "Here, stop spinning around a minute. Your bra's sticking up in the back. There. Now it's okay."

"Oh, I can't wait. I can't wait," Vi said, twirling and twirling and finally coming to a stop in front of Daddy, sitting in the club chair in his black tie and tux.

Daddy shook his head at her and smiled.

"I just love you to pieces," Vi said, reaching out a hand to him. "Smell my wrist, Harry, and tell me what you think of the perfume. It's Intrigue, and it costs a fortune."

Daddy smelled her wrist and nodded. "It's nice," he said. "I like it." Then he leaned back in the chair and said, "God, I'm pooped today."

"Oh, you always say that before the party," Vi told him. "Once we're there you'll just love it. You always do. And tonight, I'm going to really make you dance. Here, get up. Let me show you how to boogaloo. I know they're going to play 'Brown Sugar.' That's kind of their big song. I remember one time I went with my girlfriend Linda to hear them at the Live and Kicking Dance Hall on Haight, and both of us—we couldn't have been more than fifteen or sixteen—we just kept making them play it over and over again. Come on, Harry, get up."

Daddy got up slowly. "I've been exhausted all day today," he said. "I didn't sleep too well last night. I think it was all those fried shrimp I ate."

Vi grabbed his hands and pulled him around

the floor with her. By the time they left, he was laughing too and not complaining at all.

I thought Vi looked gorgeous as usual. When I was younger, there were times I would cry because I couldn't go with them to watch Vi dancing and having fun. But as I grew older, I didn't want to go. I wanted to see Vi dressed up like a fairy princess on her way to the ball and, later, be awakened to hear all about her enchanted evening.

And this year, when I was fourteen, I was having a party of my own, for the first time without Vi, the night of the dinner dance.

It was Emily's idea. Vi had been surprised at first, but then she really liked the idea. "Both of us will be able to swap stories," she said, giggling.

Grandma thought she should be at my party to supervise. She didn't like the idea of a teenage get-together without a grown-up present. Vi said no. I said no. Grandma said she could sit in Daddy and Vi's bedroom and not bother anybody, but she insisted that a grown-up should be there just in case. "Patti can look after herself," Vi said. "That's what you used to say about yourself," Grandma told her. "Are you starting in again?" Vi said. And on and on.

Grandma even spoke to Daddy, and he agreed with her for a change. Vi and I had a hard time convincing him that Grandma should not be at the party. Vi was even more determined than I. "She'd spoil everything," Vi said. "She'd keep popping in and bothering them. She'd keep bossing them around and telling them to shut up. She'd spoil everything. Patti can look after herself. Don't listen to her, Harry. She's a spoiler. You know she's a spoiler."

Finally Daddy said okay. I could have a party without Grandma on the spot, but she would telephone a few times during the evening, and if she heard anything suspicious or if I couldn't honestly swear to her that nothing was going on that shouldn't—no pot being passed around, no booze, no couples making out, no loud noises that would bother the neighbors—if I couldn't honestly swear that everything was exactly as it should be, then Grandma would have his authority to come over and tell everybody to go home. And after that, Daddy said, I'd never be trusted to have a party without a grown-up present.

Vi and I spent the afternoon rolling out pizza dough and cutting and shredding a variety of toppings that the kids would put together. She wanted to help me decorate, too, and had picked up some folded paper decorations that opened out into huge exotic orange, purple, and pink flowers.

"Emily wants to come over early and help me with the decorations," I told her.

Vi was disappointed. She wanted to see the flowers hanging all over the living room. "They'll be up when you come back," I told her. "You'll be able to see them then."

"Make sure you leave everything up," Vi said just before she left. "Don't forget."

"I won't," I told her.

After they left, suddenly, I felt scared. I didn't know why. I sat down and felt my heart beating way up in my throat. I wanted to run after my parents, I wanted to run after Vi and ask her to come back. Not to leave me alone.

Which was crazy. I'd been alone lots of times. I wasn't afraid of being alone. Why tonight, when all my friends would be over soon? Why tonight?

"It's because you're absolutely dependent on her, on your mother," Emily said when I told her. "You'd better snap out of it. You're fourteen years old, much too old to be hanging out with your mother all the time. I keep telling you it's not natural."

Emily was all in black. Black jeans, black tank top, black sandals, but a big spidery yellow chrysanthemum pinned on one side of her head. She had a lot of black eye makeup on, and her mouth was a brilliant shade of red.

"Anyway, we'd better get moving. The kids will be here soon." Emily began opening the paper flowers and arranging them all over the room. We also hung up streamers and balloons, and as we worked, I began to feel better.

"See!" Emily said as our living room exploded with colors. "Aren't we having fun? Aren't we? All by ourselves? Without her?"

"I guess so," I said. "Maybe I was just nervous because this was the first party I'd ever given by myself."

"There's nothing to it," Emily said. "I've given hundreds and all of them have been smashes."

I smiled inside but didn't answer. By this time I knew that Emily's imagination sometimes carried her away. It didn't really bother me much. She was my best friend, and best friends have to learn to shut up at times and not show the other one up.

Dan Green was the first one of the kids to arrive. "Wowee!" he said when he saw the decorations in the living room. Then he grinned, looked around, and asked, "Where's Vi?"

"Out," Emily replied. "Out for the whole evening. We have the place to ourselves."

"Oh!" Dan said, looking surprised. He never minded Vi's being around. The two of them used to laugh and kid around so much that Emily said he had a crush on her.

Grandma called about an hour after all the kids had arrived and were busy putting the pizzas together.

"Shut up, everybody!" I said. "That's my grandmother calling to check up on us."

"Why is it so quiet there?" my grandmother asked over the phone.

"They're busy making pizza," I told her.

"Where are they all?" my grandmother wanted to know.

"In the kitchen."

"All of them?"

"No. Not Joey Lee. He's in the bathroom."

"Now don't you be fresh with me, young lady," said my grandmother.

"Oh, Grandma, you know I'm not being fresh

with you. Everything's just fine, and nobody's in the bedroom. I know that's what you're worried about, but these kids aren't like that. Really, Grandma, you don't have to worry."

Grandma's voice was softer when she said, "I know you're a sensible girl, Patti. I'm not worried about you. But some of your friends. That girl, Emily . . . I just don't trust her."

"She's fine, Grandma. As a matter of fact, right now she's pulling a pizza out of the oven, and I'd better go help her."

"I'll call back in an hour," said my grandmother.

And she did. Exactly an hour later. It was nine o'clock, and all of us had finished eating and cleaning up, and were beginning to listen to some tapes and to dance.

"Don't be so quiet, everybody," I yelled out. "That's my grandmother again. Start talking and laughing but not too loud."

"What's going on there?" asked my grandmother. "What's all that noise?"

"The kids are just talking and laughing in the living room, Grandma. I'll hold up the receiver and you can listen." I waved my hands at everybody, signaling for them to talk and to laugh more quietly. Then I held up the receiver.

"Oh, don't you just love Mozart and Beethoven?" Dan said to Ryan in a silly voice, dragging him closer to the phone. Ryan got Dan's head in a headlock, so I quickly moved the phone around to another part of the room.

"I'll call you again in an hour," my grand-mother said.

"You really don't have to, Grandma," I told her. "This is all very silly. I keep telling you there is nothing to worry about. Nothing's going to happen."

"I'll call you again in an hour," my grand-mother repeated.

Dan came and stood next to me. He began making funny faces. First he pretended to be cry-ing. Then he began stretching his mouth with his fingers. I kicked out at him and tried not to laugh. "Vi and Daddy won't be home until late," I said to my grandmother. "You know they never come home before one from the dinner dance."

Dan took the hand that wasn't holding the re-ceiver and began tickling my palm.

"That's all right," my grandmother said. "I'll just keep calling until your party ends. What time are the kids going home?"

I tried to pull my hand away, but he held on.

"I don't know, Grandma. Vi said they could stay until twelve."

Dan stopped making funny faces and tickling my palm. He started smiling—a nice, friendly smile—and then he was just holding my hand.

"Twelve! She's crazy. You send them home at ten," said my grandmother. "A bunch of thirteen, fourteen-year-olds, and she says they can stay until twelve! She's so irresponsible even I can't believe it."

Dan was holding my hand and I was holding

his. It was the first time we'd ever held hands, although I'd thought about it lots of times. We were both smiling at each other too. And even though it was one of those lovely, special moments, I could still deal with my grandmother.

"Nobody's thirteen," I told her. "A couple of the kids are fifteen, and even Daddy said it was okay for everybody to stay until twelve. But Grandma, you don't have to stay up that late. You could go to sleep. If I need you, I can always call you."

Dan moved a little closer, still holding my hand. He and I were exactly the same size, and we were both smiling into each other's eyes.

"I'll call you in an hour," said my grandmother, and hung up.

Seven

I didn't speak to Grandma when she called an hour later. Vi did. She sounded angry.

"Oh, he's just been a pill all evening," I heard her say, "grumbling about everything. He didn't like the food. He got a piece of chicken breast, and he wanted a thigh. He said the wine was warm, and he argued with the waiter. Then he said he didn't feel well. Just when the dancing started, he has to feel lousy and make me go home."

Daddy had gone right off to bed, but Vi came and sat down next to Dan and me after she finished talking to Grandma. We weren't holding hands any longer, but Vi looked so angry she probably wouldn't have noticed even if we had been.

"You look gorgeous, Vi," Dan said.

She did, even though her lipstick had faded a little and her hair was beginning to droop. Her violet eyes narrowed, and she said, pouting, "This was the worst evening I ever had, thanks to your father."

"What happened?" I asked.

"Oh, he was just a deadbeat all evening. I don't know what got into him. He didn't like anything. Even when Charlie Lucas—that's another one of the senior partners," Vi explained to Dan. "Even when Charlie Lucas came over and started kidding around with us, even then he just wouldn't stop grumbling."

Vi took a deep breath. Then she began looking around the room. "Oh, those flowers! Aren't they marvelous? Didn't I tell you they would look marvelous, Patti? And I love what you did with the balloons and the streamers."

"That was Emily's idea," I told her.

Some of the kids were dancing, and Vi's feet began tapping. "I didn't get to dance at all tonight," she said in a sad little voice.

Dan stood up and held out a hand to her. "Madam," he said, "will you honor me with this dance?"

Vi giggled and jumped to her feet. I watched her as she and Dan began dancing. She shook and whirled and glittered in her fancy evening dress—a star among all the kids in their jeans and shirts. Soon she was laughing and kidding around and maybe having as good a time as she might have had at the dinner dance. I shook my head, smiled, stood up, and began repairing one of the flowers that was beginning to unravel.

Dan returned to me out of breath. Now Vi was dancing with Joey Lee. "She's such a kick," Dan said. Then he helped me with some of the other flowers that were unravelling. From time to time our hands touched and closed over each other's. Once he helped me up on a chair, his arm lingering around my waist. My happiness was so blown up inside of me I couldn't bear any more of it. I wanted the party to end. I wanted Dan to go home. Emily was giggling over in one corner with Ryan and Felissa. I wanted her to go home too. I wanted all of them to go home. I wanted to be alone with Vi so I could tell her what had happened.

The party didn't end until twelve thirty, when a few parents phoned to find out where their kids were and two others who had been waiting in their cars downstairs rang the doorbell. Vi couldn't bear for the party to end. She was having so much fun.

Her hair was down, and some of the rhinestone ornaments hung lopsided on her head. She had kicked off her shoes, and there was a Coke stain on her skirt.

"What a great party!" she said as she helped me gather up all the party remnants. "No, no, don't take them down!" as I made a movement towards the flowers. "Leave them up. Daddy will want to see them." She made a mock angry face. "Even though he was such a bad boy tonight, we'll pardon him tomorrow."

"Vi," I said. "I have to tell you something."

"What?" She was twisting her head around to look at the stain on her dress. "Now how did that happen?"

"Vi," I said, "Dan and I held hands tonight. And he said he's liked me ever since fifth grade, but he didn't think I liked him. Oh, Vi, I'm so happy."

Vi grabbed me and danced me around the room. Both of us were laughing and talking and acting crazy.

"Sit down! Sit down!" Vi said finally. "Tell me everything, from the beginning. Don't leave anything out. I knew he liked you, Patti. Didn't I always tell you he liked you? He's a real doll, that boy, a real doll!"

We sat talking until after two. Later, in bed, I couldn't sleep. I lay there thinking about how lucky I was. I wondered if Dan was also lying in his bed, thinking of me. I closed my eyes and tried to send him a message. "Dan, Dan, darling Dan," I said in my mind, "I love you, Dan." And I thought I could feel his message winging back to me. "Patti, I love you too."

What was the point in sleeping? I didn't want to waste a single precious minute. I lay there wide awake, folded up inside my joy, thinking about Dan and about how he liked me, thinking about my boyfriend, Dan, and about tomorrow, and the day after that and the day after that. . . . I heard a noise coming from the living room, and knew that Vi was also having trouble sleeping. I looked at my clock—four fifteen. I jumped out of bed and hurried inside to share some more of my happy thoughts with her.

It wasn't Vi. It was Daddy, sitting stiffly in the club chair in his bathrobe, looking pale and frightened.

"Patti," he said, "I was going to get you. Patti—something's wrong."

"What is it, Daddy?" I cried. I'd never seen him like this before. "What's wrong?"

"Shh!" he said. "You'll wake up Vi." He stiffened as he spoke, and put a hand up to his chest. "Hurts when I breathe," he said. "Hurts a lot."

He looked so frightened, I kneeled down in front of him and put my hand on his arm. "Maybe I should make you a cup of tea, Daddy," I said. "Maybe you're coming down with something."

Daddy shook his head and winced. "Call an ambulance, Patti," he said. "Right away."

I wanted to scream for help when he said that. I wanted to run and get—who? Somebody who would know what to do, because I was only a kid and I was scared.

"Heart attack," Daddy was whispering. "Hurry, Patti."

There was only me. I hurried to the phone, dialed 911, and asked them to send an ambulance right away. Then I dragged a blanket off my bed and draped it around my father. He said the pain was coming so bad he couldn't lean back or forward.

"It's going to be all right, Daddy," I told him, holding his hand, patting it, trying to keep the terror out of my voice, and control the shaking of my teeth. Every time a real bad pain hit him, he gripped my hand and I murmured something comforting. He tried to smile at me as the pains got worse, and I tried to smile back. I thought that I would go to pieces if I had to wait another minute for the ambulance to arrive.

I had to wait twelve minutes before they came. They rang the bell, and as soon as they came in, my teeth began chattering so loud I thought Daddy would hear them, that everybody would hear them, that even Vi, asleep in her bedroom, would hear them.

Nobody did. They got Daddy on a stretcher and down into the ambulance. I followed behind. They gave him oxygen and put a tube into his wrist. I sat there behind him as they worked over him, and tried to let him know I was there, and that everything would be all right.

After they took him away at the hospital, I began crying. One of the nurses came over to me, put an arm around my shoulders, and started murmuring the same kind of comforting words I'd been murmuring to my father. She said he was going to be all right, not to worry, everybody was doing everything that needed to be done, and that he was going to be all right.

I buried my head in her shoulder, and she let me cry until there was a huge wet spot on her uniform. Finally, she sat me down, gave me some water, and asked me if my father was still married. I didn't understand the question.

"I mean, are your parents divorced?"

"No, of course not. My mother's home. She's sleeping."

"I see," said the nurse, but I could see that she didn't really see. She didn't know Vi.

"I need to make a call," I told her. But I didn't have any money. I was dressed only in my pajamas and bathrobe, and when I began thinking of myself with no money, standing there in the hospital at five sixteen in the morning, and my father very, very sick, I felt so young and helpless and so frightened that I started crying all over again.

She took me into an empty office with a phone and told me to call my mother. When she left, I called my grandmother.

"Hello! Hello!" my grandmother shouted into the phone after six rings. She sounded sleepy and even more cranky than usual.

"Grandma," I said, crying, "Grandma, it's me."

"Patti? Is that you, Patti?" my grandmother said.

I was crying so hard now I couldn't answer. All I could do was sob.

"My God, Patti," my grandmother said. "What is it? What's wrong?"

"Grandma," I finally managed, "oh, Grandma, I'm at the hospital. Grandma, it's . . ."

"Oh, my God! My God!" cried my grandmother, her voice cracking with terror. "It's Vi. What happened to her? What happened?"

"No, no," I sobbed. "It's not Vi. It's Daddy. He's had a heart attack. Oh, Grandma, I'm so scared."

"Patti," said my grandmother, sounding like herself again. "Now just calm down, and tell me what happened."

I told her.

"All right then, darling," she said. "He's in good hands. The worst is over. Let me talk to Vi."

"She's not here, Grandma. She's still home. She didn't wake up. I guess she's still asleep."

"Just as well," said my grandmother, "or you'd have two patients. Now you just try to stay calm, darling. I'll be over as fast as I can. You can relax now. I'll take care of everything."

Grandma and I didn't get back to our house until nine thirty. Just twelve hours ago, I thought to myself as we walked into the quiet living room hung with the exotic paper flowers, Dan and I were holding hands and I was happier than I'd ever been in my whole life. I began crying again.

"Shh! Shh!" Grandma said. "You don't want to scare Vi. Go and wash your face and maybe get dressed. Unless you think you could sleep."

"No, no," I whispered, not crying anymore. "We have to go back to the hospital and bring some of Daddy's things. Maybe we'll be able to see him too. They said we might be able to."

"All right. Get dressed, and then we'll decide how we should handle Vi."

I washed up, put on a sweater and some jeans, and combed my hair. Grandma had some toast and tea ready for us when I joined her in the kitchen.

"I'd better tell her," I whispered to my grandmother.

"No, I think I should," said my grandmother. "I know how to handle her when she gets upset."

"We don't want to scare her," I said in a low voice. "If she gets up and sees you first, she'll be frightened. Maybe it would be better if I just went into her bedroom and told her. I'll try to just talk naturally. I won't cry anymore. I've got control over myself now."

"She'll get hysterical when you tell her," said my grandmother. "I know she will. She's scared stiff of hospitals. I remember when your Uncle Joe fell on some glass when they were kids and he cut a big gash in his leg—it needed twenty-seven stitches—and it was just gushing blood. She carried on so, you'd have thought she was the one who'd been hurt. And when you were born, we practically had to drag her into the hospital, and she was hollering so loud you could hear her two floors away. Well, never mind that now."

"Grandma," I said, "let me go in first. Let me try."

Grandma shook her head. "Okay, go ahead. I'll be here if you need me."

I tiptoed into my parents' bedroom. Vi was asleep, curled up the way she always was, her face almost covered under the blanket. I moved softly over to her side of the bed and stood there looking down at her soft, pretty hair. One of the rhinestone ornaments still glittered in her hair. I shook my head and smiled. Then I put out my arm and touched her shoulder. Vi kept on sleeping.

I sat down on the bed and whispered, "Vi." I had to say it another time before she woke up. She was smiling as her face emerged from under the blanket, even before her eyes opened. "Oh, Patti," she said, "I was having the nicest dream."

"That's nice, Vi," I said, trying to sound cheerful, "but . . ."

Vi licked her lips, and her eyes were clear and untroubled. "I dreamed that you and I were on a boat—I think it was the ferry to Sausalito—and I was dropping pieces of bread over the side, feeding the sea gulls. They were so beautiful, the sea gulls in my dream, very clean and white. And then one of them flew right onto my arm, and I just loved it, standing there on the ferry with the breeze blowing my hair and . . . and . . ." Vi yawned. "Oh, I'm so sleepy. What time is it, anyway?"

"It's nearly ten, Vi," I said, smoothing her hair and trying to look encouraging. "Now everything's just fine, but Daddy didn't feel well last night and . . ."

"Oh, right," Vi said, pulling herself up. "He was a very naughty boy." She turned to his side of the bed and then looked up at me. "Oh, he's awake already."

"Yes, he is," I said cheerfully. "He got up at night, and he didn't feel well, and then he asked me to call an ambulance, so . . ."

"A what?" Vi sat up straight.

"Now just stay calm, Vi. Daddy's fine now. He's really fine, but he had to go to the hospital because he had a heart attack. Don't get upset. He's going to be all right."

I heard the door open, and Grandma came into the room.

"No!" Vi said.

"Now, Vi," Grandma said, "just don't get yourself upset. That won't do anybody any good. Just try to—"

"No! No! No!" Vi began shouting.

"Everything's fine," Grandma said. "He's resting comfortably, so . . ."

"No!" Vi screamed. "No!"

Grandma quickly moved over to the bed and put her arms around Vi and began rocking her. "No! No! No! No! No!" Vi kept screaming, and Grandma murmured, "It's going to be all right, Vi. It's going to be all right."

Eight

Grandma and I took turns going to the hospital and looking after Vi. After a couple of days, Daddy was out of intensive care and into a regular room. He was worried about Vi, too.

"How is she doing?" he asked almost the first time he was able to speak.

"Oh, she's just fine, Daddy," I told him. "You know Vi. She's upset, but in a couple of days she'll be able to come and see you."

Daddy's face looked thinner and full of gray hollows. "It was a bad one," he said. "Don't tell Vi."

Vi didn't want to go to the hospital. "I couldn't stand seeing him if he's all hooked up. I just couldn't. And then they have all those other people there. Last time I saw a man without any legs. I couldn't stand it."

It was better for Vi when I stayed with her. After that first night, Grandma kept scolding her and preaching at her. "You just have to snap out of it now and act your age. He's your husband, and he's a very sick man, and you have to pull yourself together and go see him."

"No!" Vi kept saying. "No, I can't!"

So for the first few days that Daddy was in the hospital, Grandma and I took turns. Vi was too upset to be by herself. It was all we could do to get her out of bed and dressed. She kept crying and crying, and at first we couldn't distract her.

Mostly, she was frightened. But gradually, she began thinking about Daddy. About how he was feeling.

"Tell him I love him," Vi said one day when I was going off to the hospital and Grandma had just arrived. "Tell him I'm thinking about him all the time. Now, what can I send him? I know. I have some of those chocolate coconut cookies he likes so much in the freezer. You can bring him some of those."

"No cookies," Grandma said grimly. "He's on a strict diet now. No cookies. No fat."

Vi burst into tears again, and I shook my head angrily at Grandma. "Never mind, Vi," I told her. "I'll bring him some nice flowers from you. How about violets? Wouldn't that be a good idea? I guess I can't get real violets at this time of year, but maybe I'll buy him a pot of African violets. What color should I get?"

Vi looked up at me and stopped crying. The tears had darkened her eyelashes and made her eyes seem even larger than usual.

"What color, Vi? Should I get pink or white?"

"No, no," Vi said, sniffling. "No, no. If they're from me, get them the color of . . ."

"Of course, Vi. The color of your eyes. That's what I'll do."

Daddy shook his head and smiled when I put the big pot of violet-colored African violets down on the table next to his bed. He was sitting up in bed now and looking more like himself. Only thinner.

"She sends her love, and she wanted me to bring you some of her chocolate coconut cookies, but Grandma told her you were on a diet."

"Poor Vi," Daddy said.

"I think she'll be able to come see you in a day or so. She's really much calmer now."

"Don't push her," Daddy said. "I don't want her to get upset. You've been wonderful, Patti." His voice trembled, and he reached out a hand and took mine. "You're a wonderful daughter. I'll never forget how you handled everything when I needed you. I'll make it up to you, too, when I get well."

"Daddy," I said, "just get well. That's all I want."

"Oh, I will, I will," he said. Then he laughed. "Even your grandmother, even she's been great."

"Yes," I said, "I know. She's been doing most of the housework and the cooking."

"I know that," he said. "But I mean she's really been very nice to me. She comes every day, and she brings me things to read, and she straightens everything up in my room, and she argues with the nurses if she doesn't think I'm getting enough attention. You know what she's always thought of me."

I didn't answer.

"Well," Daddy said in an embarrassed way, "she always thought I was too old for Vi . . . among other things. . . . Anyway, I guess I haven't really been taking care of myself the way a man my age should. I've been eating like a kid, and I haven't been exercising. I'll just have to make a few changes. I hope it isn't too late."

Vi came to see Daddy on the fifth day he was in the hospital. Before starting out, she stood in front of the mirror in her bedroom, putting different outfits on and taking them off.

"Come on, Vi," I said. "You're not going to a wedding."

I must have sounded irritated, because she looked up at me, startled. "I only want to look nice for him," she said. "I want to cheer him up."

"That's right, Vi," I said patiently. "But he'll be so happy to see you, he won't care what you're wearing."

"I look terrible," Vi said. "Just look at the rings under my eyes. He'll be upset when he sees me. Maybe I shouldn't go. Maybe I should just talk to him on the phone. He always likes to talk to me on the phone."

"Vi, do what you like," I said wearily.

"You think I should go, don't you, Patti?" she said timidly.

"I think you should," I told her, "because it would do Daddy a lot of good. Daddy would be very happy if you came. He's always asking about you, but if you're going to get upset . . ."

"No, no, I'll be all right," Vi said, straightening herself out again in front of the mirror. "I'm not as bad as you think I am. But what should I wear?"

I tried to be patient with her, but I was growing tired. For five days I'd been totally buried in my father's heart attack and in Vi. I'd spoken quickly two times to Emily on the phone and once to Dan. Now that Daddy seemed out of danger, my other interests began to surface. I wanted to see my friends. Most of all, I wanted to see Dan.

"How about wearing your white sweater and your blue slacks? You could wear that blue and red jacket with the big red buttons. That's so bright."

"No, no. Something prettier. Something Daddy likes. How about my rose-colored silk blouse and gray velvet skirt?"

"Vi, you're not going to a party. People don't dress up to go to the hospital."

Finally she decided to wear a purple-and-blue flowered blouse that made her violet eyes even deeper in color, and a soft blue wool skirt.

"Daddy likes me in blues," Vi said, putting on lipstick and arching her neck to look at herself. "I need a haircut, don't I, Patti?"

"You look fine," I told her. "Can we go now?"

When we walked into the hospital, Vi put her arm through mine and huddled up closer to me as we stood waiting for the elevator. I tried to coach her on how to behave when she saw Daddy. "Don't act surprised when you see him. Remember he's thinner, and he looks a little tired. Try not to cry or look upset."

"I won't," Vi promised. "You'll see. I'll be fine."

She tightened her grip on my arm as we walked down the corridor to his room. When she saw him, sitting up in bed, watching the door eagerly, and smiling so happily as we came into the room, she let out a little cry, let go of my arm, and hurried over to him.

"Poor, poor Harry!" she said. "Poor boy!" She put her arms around him and hugged him tight.

"Not so hard, Vi," I warned. "Don't press so hard."

Daddy laughed. He pulled a little away from her, looked at her, and shook his head. "Oh, Vi," he said, "you look so beautiful. I'm so glad you came."

Vi sat down on the bed. "I just couldn't come before," she said. "I just couldn't. I was too upset. But I didn't know you were in a room all by yourself, and such a nice room, too!" She jumped up and moved over to the window. "Just look at that pretty view you have."

Daddy smiled at me, and I came over and kissed him. "How are you feeling today, Daddy?" I asked him.

"Oh, just great," he said. "I've been out of bed a couple of times already, and maybe I'll get out of bed now and sit over there in the chair."

"That's right," Vi said. "It's not good to stay in bed too long. You get weak when you stay in bed." She came over to the bed and stood there as he moved his legs over the side.

"Put on your bathrobe, Daddy," I said. "Vi, hand him his bathrobe."

Vi picked it up and handed it to him. "Why did you bring this old flannel bathrobe?" she asked me as Daddy stood up and slipped his arms into the robe. "Why didn't you bring the white silk one I bought him last Christmas?"

Daddy slowly began moving toward the chair. I hurried over to help him.

"You don't have to help him, Patti," Vi said, but I could feel him leaning on me as we walked slowly over to the chair.

"There," he said as he settled himself down and leaned carefully back. "There."

Vi was studying him, her forehead wrinkled.

"I guess I don't look so great, do I, Vi?" he said.

"Oh, no, Harry," Vi said brightly. "You look wonderful."

Daddy laughed and shook a finger at her. "Now, Vi, you don't have to lie. I know I look pretty terrible, but thank God I'm alive. I tell you that pain was so terrible I never thought I'd . . ."

"No, no," Vi said, putting her hands up over her ears. "No more about sickness. No more about bad things. From now on we're only going to talk about nice things. Look at all those pretty flowers. Aren't they beautiful? Who sent you all those pretty flowers?"

"Well, they sent me some from work, and those roses over there are from your mother."

"My mother?" said Vi. "My mother brought you flowers?"

"Yes. Isn't that something! She said she didn't pay much for them. That she got them at a stand at half price because the man was closing up and going home." Daddy laughed. "That's your mother, but anyway she brought the roses. And my secretary came with some flowers, and here's the lovely pot of violets Patti brought me. . . ."

"I told her to bring them," Vi said. "It was my idea."

"That's right," I agreed. "It was her idea. She said to get violets the color of her eyes."

"I know, sweetheart, I know," Daddy said, reaching out for Vi's hand.

"I wanted you to know I was thinking of you even though I'm such a terrible scaredy-cat about hospitals. You knew I was thinking about you, didn't you, Harry?"

Daddy began patting Vi's hand. "Of course, sweetheart, I knew."

"And you weren't disappointed because I couldn't come right away, were you? You knew I was just too upset."

"I'm never disappointed with my girl, am I?"

said Daddy. He looked up and smiled at me. "I'm never disappointed with either of my girls."

Vi took a deep, deep breath. "But now that I'm here, and I see what a nice room you have, and the nice view, and how well you are, now I'll come every day until you come home. When are you coming home anyway, Harry?"

"Oh, maybe another week or so. Soon."

Vi turned around and grinned at me. "We'll really have a party when Daddy comes home, won't we, Patti?"

"Well," I said, "maybe just the three of us. Maybe a nice, quiet celebration for just the three of us."

"We'll hang up those flowers again. Daddy never saw those beautiful flowers we had hanging up for your party, Patti."

"Oh, I saw them all right," Daddy said. "I think I can do without seeing them again."

"But when did you see them?" Vi asked. "You didn't even come into the living room when we came back from the dinner dance. I made Patti leave them up because I wanted you to see them the next day."

"Vi," I said, "he did see them. Later, when he was having his heart attack. He was sitting in the living room and he saw them. You weren't there so you didn't . . ."

"All right, all right," Vi said, waving at me to stop. "That's enough of that. From now on, we're not going to remember bad things. When your father comes home, we'll have some other kind of decorations hanging up. I'll think of something. It'll be a surprise."

Daddy twisted around in his chair.

"Are you comfortable, Daddy?" I asked. "Are you feeling all right? Is anything wrong?"

"I'm fine," Daddy said, "but maybe you can give me a pillow from my bed. This chair is a little hard."

"I'll make all the foods you like," Vi was saying. "We can have shrimp cocktails, and maybe steak and . . ."

"No," I told her, "no steak. No red meat."

Vi waved her hand at me again. "We'll figure out something. The important thing is that it's going to be a party, a special party just for Daddy."

She leaned over and kissed him on top of his head. My father smiled at her and then he smiled at me. "This is like old times. Listening to my girls planning a party. Like old times."

Nine

Dan and I biked down to Baker Beach the next day after school. The day was cool and misty, with the fog rolling across the Golden Gate Bridge. There weren't many people on the beach—some fishermen, a few dogs, their owners, and Dan and I.

At first we walked about a foot apart, trying to talk and laugh and fill in any empty spaces that might arise. This was the first time in all the years we'd known each other that we were going someplace all by ourselves.

I could feel my heart beating up in my ears, and I knew I was happy. Or rather, I knew I was supposed to be happy.

"How far do you want to walk?" Dan asked,

not looking at me, looking straight ahead. "Do you want to go to the end?"

"Sure," I said, looking down at my shoes. "Maybe we'll be able to see some tide pools."

"Tide pools!" Dan laughed. "I never saw any tide pools there."

Both of us began laughing nervously because we knew that the far end of the beach was often occupied by nudists. We drew a little closer, and I said, "Well, I go there to look at the tide pools. I can imagine what *you* go there to look at."

"Sure, sure," Dan said. "You're just interested in tide pools. Sure."

It wasn't all that witty a comment, but I began laughing so hard that for the first time in my life, I could feel the tears welling up in my eyes. Just like Vi!

Dan moved even closer so that our shoulders brushed together as we walked. He was laughing too. As soon as I could pull myself together, I gasped, "I'll show you when we get down there. I'll show you. . . ."

"What?" Dan shouted. "What will you show me?"

"The anemones in the tide pools, you big jerk," I howled, pushing him hard. He pushed me back, and for a while we tussled together. When we stopped, we began walking again, holding hands, and now I knew I was happy.

"Do you really go to look at tide pools?" Dan asked, turning to smile into my face. His eyes were a deep, deep shade of brown, and his hair was dark brown, too.

"Yes, I do. In seventh grade, Mrs. O'Reilly, my science teacher, brought us all down during a low tide. It was a cold day, so there weren't any people—any nude people—around. Emily and I have come down a couple of times too." I didn't tell him that I'd also been down once with Vi, but that she was so distracted by the nudists, and got so giggly and silly, that we didn't really have much chance to look at the tide pools that day.

We began swinging our hands. Dan said, "Emily's a funny girl."

"Yes," I said, "I know. But she's very intelligent."

"Oh, I know that," Dan said. "Everybody knows that. She makes sure everybody knows it."

"She's a good friend," I said, thinking how good my hand felt inside his.

"I've got nothing against her," he said. "She's your friend, and that's enough for me. Watch out there!"

The fishermen had their poles standing upright further back on the sand, and the lines were nearly invisible as they passed right in front of us into the water.

He dropped my hand to curl his arm around my shoulders, protecting me, guiding me away from the lines. It felt good having his arm around me, and I must have moved inside of it in such a way to signal to him that I liked it there. He tightened his arm around me, and we continued walking that way.

Cool, wet breezes blew into our faces as we moved along the gray, misty beach. There was a shimmering, white light on the sand, on the waves, and in the sky that made me tremble suddenly with pleasure.

"Are you cold, Patti?" Dan asked, pulling me closer to him.

"No," I told him, "but it's all so beautiful down here. I mean the colors. Most people like it when it's sunny, but there's something . . . something special . . ." I couldn't finish but Dan nodded.

"Yes," he said, "I know what you mean."

That day it was too cold for any nudists to be out, and the tide wasn't low enough for us to scramble over the rocks to look for tide pools. The beach ended up against a deserted elbow of sand and rock.

"Do you want to turn back?" Dan asked.

"No," I told him. "Let's sit over there and look at the ocean."

We fitted ourselves into a rocky crook, huddling together, with Dan's arm still around my shoulders. I reached out and took his hand, and he said, "I really like you a lot, Patti."

"I know," I said. "I like you too."

"Everybody likes you," he said. "I guess just about every guy I know has a crush on you."

"I don't believe that," I said. "I never thought anybody liked me."

"Come on," he said. "You're the prettiest girl in school." Then he added. "And the nicest."

The prettiest girl? I never thought of myself as the prettiest girl. Vi always said I was pretty, and lately, when I looked at myself in the mirror, I liked what I saw. But the prettiest girl? No, I wasn't the prettiest girl. I didn't want to be the prettiest girl. It was wonderful having a whole bunch of great kids like me, and I knew they all liked me, but I didn't want it to be because I was pretty.

"No!" I said. "I'm not."

"And it's fun being around you. You're always so . . . so . . . not like Emily. You always have to notice her or she gets sore. I mean, I like her. She's your friend so she's okay with me. But you're not like that. You're fun to be around. And it's fun at your house, too. I always heard about the great parties you always had at your house. Even when we were kids. You didn't notice me then, but I sure noticed you."

"But you never acted like you were noticing me. You never said anything to me."

"I guess I was shy," Dan said. "But I always hoped you'd have a party and invite me."

"I didn't usually invite boys until I was thirteen," I told him. "That's why I didn't invite you."

"You invited Noah Bernstein," he said, "when you were thirteen. He told everybody you were his girlfriend."

"I was not," I said. "I never was."

"Well, he's a pretty nice guy," Dan said generously.

"No, he's not." I leaned my head on his shoulder. "Compared to you, he's nothing."

I could feel Dan's face in my hair. "I don't know," he said. "He's not so bad."

"I didn't even invite him to the Halloween party this year," I said.

"You invited me this year," Dan said. "I loved it. I loved the party. I loved your house. You've got the greatest house. And your mother—well, your mother is great too. You're just like her."

"Me? Like Vi?"

"Yes. You're pretty the way she is. And you're fun and a good sport."

I pulled my head up off his shoulder. No, I thought, no. I don't want to be pretty like Vi. I don't want to be like Vi at all. It made me angry, all of a sudden, that Dan thought I was like Vi. It made me say spitefully, "Emily said you have a crush on her."

"On Vi? On your mother?" Dan said. "That's crazy."

"Well, that's what Emily said."

"I don't want to talk about Emily." Dan tightened his fingers on my shoulders. Then, each of us moved towards the other, and we kissed, and I wasn't angry at him anymore.

We must have sat there another hour or so, watching the setting sun turning the gray mists into pinks and reds. Little sandpipers strutted along the shore, and white gulls and cormorants flew overhead.

"Do you ever want time to stop?" I asked him. "Do you ever feel you want to be frozen in a certain moment when everything is perfect?"

"Like now?" Dan said. "I know what you mean, but no, I don't want time to stop, because I know everything is going to get even better and better."

It grew so cold that suddenly the two of us

were freezing, even huddled together as we were. We jumped up and hurried back to our bikes, marveling at the rosy red colors of sunset all around us.

When we reached my house, it was already dark.

"Well," I said to him, "well . . ."

"I guess I should go," he said. "I guess Vi will be looking for you."

"Oh, no," I said, not wanting him to go, not wanting it to end. "Unless your mother will be worried about you."

"She doesn't worry about me. She knows I can take care of myself."

We were both holding our bikes and standing in front of my building. People were coming in and out, and we moved ourselves and our bikes over to one side to be out of the way.

"I've never met your mother," I said. "I've never met your father either."

I was beginning to realize that Dan was not alone, that he was part of some other world as well as mine.

"They're okay," he said. "My father is a cop, but he's a real nice guy. He actually works in an office now—he keeps crime statistics. He's nothing like the cops on 'Hill Street Blues.' "

"Does he have a gun?"

"Well, sure, but he never has to use it. My grandfather was a cop too, and so is one of my uncles. It sort of runs in the family."

"You don't want to be a cop, do you?"

"I don't know," Dan said. He had a way of

licking his upper lip with his tongue and nodding slightly when he was thinking, which I noticed. There were lots of things I was noticing about him. "I might. I guess my dad expects me to, but I think it would be more interesting to work for the F.B.I."

"But that's dangerous. Doesn't your mother mind that your father is a cop, and that you're thinking about working for the F.B.I.?"

Dan propped his bike up against the building. I did the same, and then we held hands and leaned against our bikes. It felt very comfortable.

"Maybe," he said. "I guess she's happy that he's doing crime statistics now, but she's not worried about me. She's much more worried about my sister Lorrie."

"You have a sister?"

"I have two sisters. One is Lorrie. She's sixteen and a half, and my mother worries about her all the time. The other one, Mollie, is only eight. She's a pain in the neck, but nobody has to worry about her. She's a real tough little egg. She can beat up any boy in her class, and usually does."

Dan laughed, and I did too. Even though I didn't actually know his sister Mollie or any of the other people in his family, I felt that I was now a part of Dan's world just as he was a part of mine.

"My mother's okay," Dan said. "She screeches and nags a lot, but she's harmless. I guess she's like most mothers. She's certainly not like yours. Not like Vi."

"What do you mean?"

"Well, Vi is more like a friend than a mother. You really are lucky. Most kids' mothers you have to act a way that you're not. The way a kid is supposed to act in front of a grown-up. It's phony and it's not much fun, and usually I don't like it if a parent hangs around. But it's different with Vi. You can tell her anything and kid around with her. She's like another kid. And she's such a good sport, too. And fun! Man, is she fun! You sure are lucky."

"She went to pieces after my father had his heart attack," I said sharply.

"Well, I guess anyone would," Dan said. "Poor Vi, it must have been a terrible shock."

"How about your mother?" I asked angrily. "Would she go to pieces if your father had a heart attack?"

"I don't know, Patti," Dan said smiling, not noticing my anger. "He never did. But she is a nurse, and she's used to things like that. My sisters and I were always breaking bones, and once my father cracked a few ribs." Dan shook his head. "Not in the line of duty either. He just tripped on the stairs and went flying. Boy, was he a mess. At first it looked like he'd broken his nose, too, there was so much blood."

"But what happened to your mother?"

"Oh, she was home. We all were home when it happened."

"Did she crack up?"

"My mother? No, she's pretty cool when there's trouble. She calmed him down. She calmed us all down. Then, after she stopped the bleeding, she got him into the car and drove him to the hospital. But she's a nurse. She's used to it. Not like Vi. She's so . . . well . . . kind of tender . . . how is she, anyway? I should have asked you about her. And your father too? I should have asked you first thing, but I guess I got distracted."

He pulled me over to him, and for a while we both forgot about that other world out there.

"Do you want to come up?" I asked him finally. "Vi would be glad to see you. She went to the hospital today by herself because my father looks better. He's really had a very serious heart attack, but she doesn't know it yet. Anyway, can you come up? Is it too late?"

"No. We're pretty laid back at home. I'd like to come up."

When we opened the door to the apartment, we could hear the stereo going and we could smell something good coming from the kitchen.

"Vi," I called, "it's me."

Vi came running out of the kitchen. Her cheeks were rosy, her hands full of flour, and she was grinning.

"Hi, Patti," she cried. "Oh, hi there, Dan. How nice to see you!"

"Hi, Vi," Dan said. "How is your husband? How is Mr. Carmichael?"

"Oh, he's just great. Just wonderful. I don't even know why they're keeping him. We had such fun today, Patti. I brought one of our old photo albums, and we sat there looking at some of the old pictures, and then when this silly doctor came in to check him over and I got out of the way fast, I started talking to a woman in the next room, a real doll. She had to have some kind of knee surgery, and she and I just started talking and kidding around, and she said I really made her day. She's so bored hanging around there with nobody to talk to. Maybe tomorrow when I go to see Daddy, I'll bring her some brownies. That's what I'm making now. And Patti, Grandma is staying late at the hospital tonight, so she won't be coming here for dinner. We can eat anything we like. I picked up some hot sausages, and I thought we'd make sausages and peppers. She hates hot sausages. You can stay for dinner too, Dan, if you like. Oh, why don't you stay for dinner? We'll have a lot of fun if you do."

"I guess I can," Dan said. "I'll call home and tell them."

While Dan was phoning, Vi put her arms around me and kissed me a couple of times. "I feel so great, Patti," Vi said. "I see now I was just worrying over nothing. Daddy's fine. He'll be as good as new when he comes home, and things will just go on the same as ever."

"He's had a heart attack, Vi," I said. "He's going to have to be careful."

Vi turned up the volume of the stereo. "Sometimes, Patti, you sound just like your grandmother," she said.

Ten

Daddy came home early in March. I had to keep talking and talking before Vi understood that his homecoming was not a proper occasion for a party.

"Just the three of us," she kept insisting. "Well"—making a face—"I guess your grandmother, too. I wasn't planning on inviting anybody else."

"No," I said. "He's not supposed to have any excitement."

"I thought I could have the florist make up a centerpiece of spring flowers. You know, Patti, with tulips and daffodils and irises. And maybe I'll make a turkey with corn bread stuffing, like for Thanksgiving, because we're so thankful he's coming home."

"Vi," I said, "let's just forget about a party now. Let's just keep it nice and peaceful for him. Flowers aren't good for him, either. He started wheezing a few days ago, and the doctor says it's not good for him to sleep in a room with flowers."

"I didn't know that," Vi said. "Nobody told me that."

"Because you never talk to the doctor," I said. "Either he talks to Grandma or he talks to me. If you want to talk to him, you shouldn't run out of the room when he comes to examine Daddy. Or you could call him. He's really a nice guy, for a doctor."

"No," Vi said, waving her hand. "I don't want to talk to the doctor. I hate doctors."

"Well, you should talk to this one," I said impatiently. "He'll tell you Daddy will need to rest a lot."

Vi brightened up. "I know," she said. "I'm going to buy some new sheets and pillowcases. I saw some at one of those fancy specialty stores downtown—beautiful snow-white ones with eyelet embroidery and lace on the cases. They were gorgeous. And expensive too. But Daddy won't mind." She looked at her watch, and began wailing. "Oh, it's too late now. And tomorrow I have to pick him up at eleven. There won't be enough time."

"That's all right, Vi," I said, speaking slowly. "Why don't you use those blue sheets with the pretty flower design? You know how much

Daddy loves blue. I'll help you make the bed in the morning before we go to the hospital."

Vi smiled and nodded. "That's good, Patti. And I'm glad you're not going to school tomorrow. I thought I'd have to go get Daddy all by myself."

"But didn't Grandma say she was going to meet you there?"

"Oh, her!" Vi said, giving me her conspiratorial smile. "She doesn't count."

"She's been wonderful. Even Daddy says so."

"I wish she'd stay home," Vi said. "She's so bossy. She's always telling me how to act with Daddy—as if I didn't know how to take care of my own husband."

"Well, Vi, he has had a heart attack and . . ."

"Stop it, Patti!" Vi said, shaking her head. "I don't know what's gotten into you lately. You're not like yourself."

Before I could answer, Vi suddenly burst out laughing. "I know what. Let's run over to Stonestown," she said. "There's that one store that has marvelous artificial flowers. I'll get a bunch of pink and red silk roses and maybe some of those big fake white spider chrysanthemums, and we can put them in the bedroom, and maybe pick up a few colorful pillows. He'll like that. We'll make the bedroom look like a harem. Maybe I can buy one of those little Persian-type carpets. Oh, yes, that's what I'll do."

Daddy didn't notice the flowers or the pillows or the rug when he arrived home. He was so tired, he went right to bed and fell asleep.

Grandma, Vi, and I sat around the kitchen talking in low, worried voices. Or rather Grandma and I talked in low, worried voices.

"I don't like the way he looked this morning," Grandma said. "I don't think his color was very good."

"He didn't eat much breakfast," I said. "He said he wasn't hungry."

"Nowadays," my grandmother whispered angrily, "they push you out of the hospital almost before you get in. It's a disgrace. Years ago, when I had my babies, you stayed in the hospital for at least five or six days. Now they send you home the next day. I told the doctor and that fat little nurse, too, that I thought he wasn't well enough to come home."

"Maybe I should go and listen outside his door. Maybe there's something he wants," I said.

"Don't make any noise," said my grandmother. "Don't startle him."

Later in the afternoon, when Daddy woke up, he said he felt fine. He got up out of bed and came and sat down in his old chair in the living room. You could see he had lost a lot of weight while he was in the hospital. He looked thinner, older, and almost too small for the big club chair.

"Just don't overdo it," said my grandmother. "Take it easy."

"Oh, I will, Eva, I will," said my father, leaning his head back on the chair.

Eva? I'd never heard him call my grandmother Eva. I'd never heard him address her directly by name. She was always "your grandmother" when he spoke of her to me or "your mother" when he spoke of her to Vi.

"How about something to eat?" said Vi. "Are you hungry?"

"I'd like a cup of tea," said my father. "I don't feel like eating anything just yet."

Vi jumped up. "I'll get you some tea," she said, "and maybe a few cookies."

"No cookies," said my grandmother sternly. "And no black tea. He needs to drink herb tea."

"Herb tea?" Vi looked puzzled.

"I brought a few boxes over the other day and put them into the cupboard. Peppermint, Sleepytime, and chamomile. I told you, but I guess you didn't hear me. I'll go make a pot."

My grandmother moved off to the kitchen, and Vi stood there, her forehead all scrunched up.

"Come over here, Vi, and sit near me," Daddy said. "I can't tell you how good it is to be home."

Vi sat down on the chair next to his. "I hated it when you were in the hospital," she said, pouting. "I hated it."

My father reached over and took her hand. "Poor little Vi!" he said.

Vi gave his hand a playful tap. "You've been a very, very bad boy," she told him. "Don't ever do it again."

He shook his head at her, and I got up and hurried into the kitchen. "Can I help you, Grandma?" I asked.

"No, no, I'm fine. Later, I'll make him some soup. Something light. And maybe I'll make some apple sauce, too. But now I'll just give him a cup of herb tea."

"If you don't need me, Grandma, maybe I can go and make a call."

"Go ahead, Patti," my grandmother said, smiling at me. "I'm here if he needs anything."

I hurried into my room and called Dan. Nobody answered. It was four fifteen, and I wondered where he was. It was still hard for me to think of him involved in a life that didn't have me at its center. Where could he be? I felt annoyed, and when I heard Vi's laughter, I got up and closed the door. Then I called Emily.

She answered on the first ring.

"It's me," I told her.

"Me who?" she said, giggling into the phone. I could hear somebody behind her saying something and then she started laughing and kept on laughing. It was so irritating that I hung up.

She called right back. "What's with you?" she said.

"Oh, nothing," I said. "Everything's just great. Just wonderful."

"What is it, Patti?" She sounded very serious. She sounded the way a friend is supposed to sound when she's worried about you. I felt stupid.

"I guess I'm just kind of tense," I said. "My father's home."

"Oh!" Emily said. I heard a voice further back in the room, a boy's voice, and she said, covering up the phone, "Just give me a few minutes. It's Patti. Go read a book or something."

"Who's there?" I asked her.

"Oh," she said, beginning to giggle again, "it's . . . somebody . . ."

I knew who it was. I knew it was Dan. My Dan. No, not my Dan anymore. He was over at Emily's house, and that's why he hadn't been at his own house when I called. The two of them had been laughing and kidding around, and what else had they been doing? Emily had always liked Dan, and even though he said he didn't like her, he always kept talking about her. Now I knew why. He loved her. He was finished with me. I'd lost him, and I'd lost her too. I began sobbing.

Emily stopped giggling again. "What is it, Patti? What's wrong? Is your father all right?"

I didn't answer. I didn't hang up either. I just held the phone and kept sobbing into it. My whole world was suddenly disintegrating, and I didn't know what to do next.

"Patti, Patti, say something. Patti! Do you want me to come over? I'll get rid of Alex, and I'll be right over. Patti!"

Alex?

"Alex?" I gasped.

"Alex. You know. Alex Chapin. The guy in my algebra class. The one who's been helping me with my homework. Oh, I guess you don't know. But Patti, what is it? What's wrong?"

"Nothing," I said. "Nothing's wrong."

"Is your father all right? Do you want me to come over?"

What a friend Emily was! Dan wasn't at her

house after all. He didn't love Emily, my best friend, Emily. Dan loved me, and Emily was happy because a boy named Alex Chapin was helping her with her algebra homework.

"He's all right," I said, "and I am too. But I just couldn't help crying. I don't know why," I lied.

"No wonder," Emily said. "You've been under terrible pressure. My mother was just saying last night that people forget how hard sickness is on the families of an invalid. She even gives a workshop at one of the hospitals for families who have a sick relative."

"She does?"

"Yes. So don't feel ashamed. If you want to cry, go on and cry. You've listened to me cry lots of times."

"Emily," I said, "you're my best friend. I'm so happy I have you for my best friend. Now what's with Alex?"

"I can't talk now," she said in a low voice. "I'll call you later, though."

"Okay," I said. "Make sure you do."

When I hung up, I continued sitting in my room.

"Patti," I heard my grandmother call. "Do you want a cup of herb tea?"

"No," I said, and then added, "I'm going to get started on my homework."

But I didn't get started on my homework. I just continued sitting on my bed, thinking about Emily, my best friend, Emily, and hungering for her. I hadn't seen her for days and days, and I wanted to see her, to be with her. I wanted to see Dan. Most of all, I wanted to get out of my house.

The phone rang, and I picked it up.

"Hello," Dan said.

"Oh, Dan," I told him, breathlessly, "I just tried to call you, but you weren't home."

"I just got in," he said. "How's your father?"

"Kind of tired. He doesn't look well. My grandmother and I think he should have stayed in the hospital longer."

"How's Vi?"

"Oh, Vi," I said. "She's herself."

"Well, that's good," he said. "I guess you're going to be busy tonight?"

"Yes," I said. "No, no, I'm not. Listen, Dan, can you meet me? I mean right away?"

"Well, I guess so. Sure. I was supposed to go to the library, but it can wait."

"That's okay," I told him. "How about if I meet you there? I can tell my folks I have to go to the library for school. That would be great. I can be there in fifteen minutes. I'll take a bus."

"It may take me a little longer," he said.

"I'll wait," I told him. "I just have to get out. Right away. I'll see you soon."

I hung up and quickly inspected myself in the mirror. I didn't care what I looked like, but I knew I looked good. Lately, I always looked good.

My father and grandmother were drinking herb tea in the living room.

"Where's Vi?" I asked.

"She's making herself a cup of *black* tea," my grandmother said.

"Well, I think I'm just going to run over to the library. I have a lot of schoolwork I have to catch up on," I lied. "But of course if you really need me . . ."

"No, no," said my grandmother. "You don't want to fall behind in your work. Just don't stay out too late. We'll probably have dinner about six."

"Don't wait for me," I said. "I'll grab something later."

Vi came into the room, carrying a cup of tea and a plate of cookies. "Where are you going, Patti?" she asked. "Don't you want any cookies?"

"I'm going to the library, and no, I don't want any cookies."

"Just wait a few minutes until I have my tea, and I'll drive you."

"No, I don't want you to drive me, Vi. I'm in a big hurry. I'll see you all later."

Vi started to say something, but I pretended I didn't hear her and hurried off.

Dan and I sat in one corner of the library and talked in low voices.

"Would you like me if I . . ." I wanted to say if I weren't pretty, but that sounded so conceited, I had to find another way to put it.

"If you what?" Dan asked. My hand was lying on the table, and he slid his own hand over it. Both of us looked around the room. The librarian was sitting at the information desk with her back to us. There was only one other person in that part of the library—an old man who was dozing over a copy of *Playboy.*

"If I were . . . if I were ugly, really ugly?"

"It wouldn't be you if you were ugly," Dan whispered, smiling at me. He eyes roamed over my face and my hair.

"No, Dan, I mean—maybe not ugly, but if I didn't look like me. If I looked different?"

"It wouldn't be you." He pressed my hand and whispered, "Just the way you are is perfect with me."

"But if I were in an accident, and my face were scarred, it would still be me."

"Yes," he said, "I guess it would be. But you're not going to be in an accident. I won't let you be in an accident."

The librarian looked up at the clock and stood up. Dan pulled away his hand just before she turned in our direction. "The library will be closing in ten minutes," she said.

I needed more time than that to explain what I meant to Dan. Maybe I also needed more time to explain what I meant to myself.

Eleven

Emily brought Alex over to our table in the lunchroom the next day. There was a brightness about her, a way she had of speaking quickly, laughing suddenly at something he had said, and of looking proudly at him that told everybody how she felt.

On the phone the night before, Emily insisted she had spoken to me about Alex ages ago.

"No, you didn't," I said. "I thought you liked Ryan Kingman. You always said you did."

"I never liked him. I only said he was okay until somebody better came along."

"Emily, I remember right around the time my father got sick, you told me you were going to ask Ryan to go to the movies with you. You said you thought he liked you. You can't deny you said that."

"Well, so what?" Emily said. "So I asked him, and he said no, as a matter of fact. I never got around to telling you that, because your father got sick. But don't you remember how I told you there was this real smart kid in my algebra class who stuttered a little . . . ?"

"No, I don't remember."

"I know I told you because my teacher, Mrs. Curry, kept saying how dumb everybody in the class was except for Alex. And then he offered to stay after school and tutor any kids who needed tutoring, and how I was the only one who showed up. I told you."

"No, you didn't."

"Well, anyway, that was a few weeks ago. Maybe you forgot because of what happened with your father."

"I didn't forget because you never told me."

"Okay, okay. Let's start all over again. Alex has been tutoring me for a few weeks, and I've really improved in math."

"I could have tutored you," I said. "I didn't know you were even having trouble." Suddenly I heard myself and hated what I was hearing. What was the matter with me anyway? So what if Emily hadn't told me about the trouble she was having with algebra or liking Alex, either, for that matter. So what? Did I tell her everything? Why was I so jealous? Why? My father's illness had changed everything, I realized. For all the time that my own life had been so wrapped up with him, other people's lives had gone on without me. Emily's, for instance. She wasn't frozen in time, waiting for me to return and be a part of her life again. Just as Dan had a life that didn't always include me, so did Emily.

"I'm sorry, Emily," I mumbled. "I sound like a real creep."

"It's okay," Emily said breezily, eager to get on with the details of her story. Emily had changed since my father's heart attack. There was an ache inside of me, knowing that I'd had no part in that change, but I shut up and listened.

"So anyway, he really helped me understand algebra, but I could see he was very shy. He doesn't talk much because he stutters. Even in class, when he knows the answers, he hardly ever raises his hand, because he's ashamed of his stutter. And you know, Patti, I'm kind of shy, too."

"Yes," I said, "I know." And I did. In spite of all her boasting and bragging, I'd come to know that basically Emily was shy. But it was strange hearing her admit it.

"I figured I'd have to be the one who made the first move, because I really liked him. I liked how intelligent he was and how—well, sweet."

"So, what did you do?"

"I asked him to come over to my house and help me with my homework there. I told him we'd be more comfortable than in the classroom, and he . . . he . . . he got very red."

"Red?"

"His face really got red, and I thought he was going to say no like they always do."

"Oh, Emily!" I said. "You never told me."

"Well, I never wanted to admit it, but boys have never liked me. Even worse, they don't usually even notice me. So it's been rough. Especially with a friend like you."

"What do you mean, a friend like me?"

"You know what I mean, Patti."

"No, honest, I don't."

"Everybody likes you. Girls too. And you're so pretty. I know I'm not pretty."

"No," I said. "No. I don't want to be pretty. It's not important being pretty."

"Don't be a nut," Emily said. "Everybody wants to be pretty. Anyway, Alex got very red, so I said, 'Well, if you don't want to . . .' But he said, 'Yes,' as quickly as he can say anything. 'Yes, I want to. But I was going to ask you to come to my house.'" Emily laughed. "It was so funny. So wonderful. He liked me too, and he said he'd been afraid it was all going to end because he realized I didn't really need any more tutoring, that I understood algebra, and he was trying to figure out what to do next. Oh, he's really great. Even my mother thinks so."

"Your mother?"

"Uh-huh. And you know what a snob she is. But even she thinks he's very intelligent. And he's involved in politics. During the mayoral election last fall, he said he went around ringing doorbells even though he hates having to talk to strangers. Sometimes he says they didn't have much patience and slammed the door before he even managed to finish a sentence. I'll bring him around tomorrow at lunch to meet you and the kids. You, he knows. Everybody knows you. But I want him to meet Dan and . . . and"—Emily laughed—"and Ryan too."

Alex was a tall, thin boy with an ordinary face. He wasn't good looking, and he wasn't bad looking. Until you got to know him, the thing you noticed most about him was his stutter.

"I'm sorry about your father," Alex said to me. Only it took him a while to say it. The word *father* was the hardest. You could see him struggling over it, controlling his embarrassment, and finally getting it out. How easy it was for me, I realized, to speak. How easy it was for most people.

"Thanks," I said quickly, and wondered what to say next.

Emily was talking loudly to the other kids, pretending not to notice Alex and me talking. But I knew she was noticing and hoping we were going to hit it off.

Dan, sitting next to me on my other side, asked me in a low voice if I wanted to go outside with him before the next period.

"In a few minutes," I told him, and turned back to Alex. He was looking straight ahead, and I could feel his shyness reaching out to me.

"I hear you're good in math," I said brightly. Alex turned red, but then I began smiling and so did he. We were going to be friends. "So what do you think?" I continued. "Will Emily be another

Einstein?" Both of us laughed out loud, and Emily stopped talking and looked at us, smiling.

"What did you just say?" she asked eagerly.

I stood up and said to Emily and Alex, "Dan and I are going outside for a while. Do you guys want to come?"

I could see Emily liked it when I said "you guys." Alex liked it too, because he stood up, turned to her, and said, "Coming?"

Only Dan didn't like it. He was quiet as the four of us sat together on the steps outside the main entrance. Emily and I did most of the talking, but even Alex spoke up more than Dan. Especially when I asked him how come he was so active in politics.

"Because it's important," he said.

"Lots of things are important," I told him. "Why politics?"

"It's important to me," he said. "I don't like feeling helpless. If I just sat around doing nothing and some joker got elected who messed up, I'd feel much worse knowing I didn't do anything to stop him."

"I don't know," Emily said, her face shining. You could tell she was proud of him even though he had to struggle so hard to speak. "I think I'd feel worse knowing I couldn't stop him. That would make me feel helpless."

The two of them began arguing then. Emily threw back her head and insisted she was right. Alex stuttered and stammered, but he wouldn't back down.

"Hey!" Emily yelled suddenly, "We're going to be late. Let's go!" She and Alex ran off together.

Dan said to me, "Let's cut next period."

"I can't," I told him. "It's my Spanish class, and we're having a test."

"Well, can we meet after school and go somewhere—by ourselves?"

"Great," I told him. "I don't have to be home early. My grandmother's there."

"Don't ask Emily," Dan said as we hurried along the hall. "I can't stand that friend of hers."

I didn't have a chance to say anything then because the bell had already rung, but later, as we walked along together towards Lincoln Park, I asked him, "Why don't you like Alex?"

"Because he's a weirdo," Dan said, slipping an arm around my shoulder. It was beginning to feel natural, having his arm around my shoulder. Even though we passed kids on the street whom we knew, I didn't mind that they saw us walking like that. I was happy that they saw us, and knew that Patti loves Dan and Dan loves Patti.

"He's not a weirdo," I said strongly, but I still managed to nestle comfortably under Dan's arm into his side. He tightened his fingers on my shoulder. "I like him. I think he's very intelligent."

"Well, so what if he's intelligent? So's Emily. They don't always have to be showing off, do they? They don't always have to act like they're better than everybody else."

"Dan," I cried in surprise, "you're jealous of him."

Dan pulled his arm off my shoulder. "Jealous?" he repeated. "Jealous of that creep? Are you kidding? He's in my P.E. class, and the guy is such a marshmallow he can't even run around the block the way everybody else has to."

"So what if he can't run around the block," I said, moving myself stiffly away from him. "That doesn't make him any the less intelligent or you any the less jealous of him."

"You're crazy, Patti," Dan said angrily. "Why should I be jealous of him?"

"I don't know," I told him. "Maybe because he is so intelligent. Sometimes I feel jealous of Emily, so I can understand. I guess I know I'm not as smart as she is and I'd like to be."

"Big deal!" Dan said. "So what if she is smart? But how somebody like you could ever be jealous of somebody like Emily . . ." He hit his forehead with his hand.

"And how somebody like you could ever be jealous of somebody like Alex . . ." I repeated, hitting my forehead with my hand.

Then both of us stopped walking, turned to look at each other, and smiled.

"Our first fight," I said proudly.

"You're crazy," he said, grabbing me and shaking me around.

Afterwards, we continued walking, with his arm around my shoulders and me nestling up again inside of it.

"We're both good looking," I told him.

"You are," he said. "You're beautiful."

"Well, you're pretty gorgeous yourself," I said.

Dan pushed me with his hip, and I pushed him with mine. We tussled a little before we continued walking again.

"Would you like me if I was intelligent?" I asked him.

"You are intelligent," he said.

"No, I mean if I was really smart like Emily."

"Yuck!" Dan said.

The day was warm and full of bright sunshine. The two of us flopped down on the grass in the park and exchanged a few kisses before I picked up the thread of the conversation.

"Did you ever think it could be a curse being good looking?" I asked him.

Dan pulled up some grass and threw it on my head. "Now you're not so good looking," he said.

I giggled and threw some grass back at him. "That's enough," I told him. "Let's talk. I really want to say this. I guess I was trying to say it yesterday. But when you're good looking, it's enough for some people. They don't expect any more. And it's not fair. And it's not good for you, either, if nobody expects anything from you."

"I expect a lot from you," Dan said, rolling me around on the grass. We never did finish the conversation, but I didn't really mind. I liked him so much, and there would be plenty of other times to talk seriously.

Even before I opened the door to my house, I could hear Vi's voice. "Patti, where have you been?" She came hurrying towards me as I entered the hallway. "I've been waiting and waiting for you." I looked at her in surprise. I'd forgotten about her. I'd forgotten about my father, too. I'd been having such a good time I'd forgotten about everything. My stomach lurched as I realized that I was home and that I didn't want to be home.

"I had some homework," I said quickly. "So I stayed late at school."

Vi was looking at my jacket. I followed the path of her eyes and saw the blades of grass sticking to it. "Then later," I said, "Dan and I went off to the park for a little while."

Vi smiled. "Oh, that's nice, Patti. I'm glad you were having fun. I just didn't know where you were. Usually you call when you're going to be late."

"Well, maybe you shouldn't be expecting me right after school anymore. Maybe you should just figure I'm busy with my schoolwork or my friends."

"Patti," Vi said, "let's get out for a while. I need to run a few errands, and you can come with me."

"Gin!" I heard my father shout from the kitchen, and my grandmother began laughing.

"What's going on in there?" I asked.

Vi made a face. "They're playing gin rummy. Most of the day he's been sleeping, and she made me go tiptoeing around the house. Then when he woke up, she taught him gin rummy. He never played any card games before. He always hated cards. I wish she'd go home and leave us alone."

"Is that you, Patti?" My grandmother came out of the kitchen, smiling. "How are you, darling?"

"Just fine, Grandma. How's Daddy?"

"He's a real killer," said my grandmother. "I just taught him how to play gin, and he's killing me."

"Beginner's luck, Eva," Daddy said, coming out of the kitchen. "How's school, Patti?"

I moved over to give him a kiss. "How are you feeling, Daddy?"

"Terrible," he said. "Your grandmother is turning me into a gambler."

"I want to get out," Vi said in a cranky voice. "Let's go, Patti."

"I think I'd better stay home, Vi. I have some homework to do, and I want to give Grandma a hand."

Grandma shook her head. "Everything's done, Patti. Dinner's all cooked. Nothing to do."

"Come on, Patti," Vi pleaded. "I've been stuck in all day. Come on out with me."

"That's right," Daddy said. "Why don't you go out with Vi, Patti? She's been in all day, and she needs to get out. As a matter of fact, why don't both you girls have dinner out? Maybe go to a movie. How would you like that, Vi?"

Vi's face sparkled. "Okay, Patti?" she asked.

"Well, what about Daddy?"

"I'll give Harry his dinner," my grandmother said. "And then he should get into bed and relax. Maybe watch a little TV. Go to bed early. But I'll stay until you get back."

"I haven't been out for dinner with Patti for ages," Vi said.

"I don't think I should," I said solemnly. "I've

really got a lot of homework to do. But, Vi, why don't you go by yourself?"

"I don't want to go by myself," Vi said, pouting.

"Go with her, Patti," my father said. "Please."

What could I do if he asked me that way? Vi hurried off to put on some makeup, and my grandmother whispered to me that Vi was acting like a spoiled brat and that maybe I should tell her to straighten herself out and think of her sick husband.

But I didn't. We went to the Courtyard for dinner, and Vi kept trying to get me to tell her about Dan. I didn't want to tell her about Dan or about anything else. I didn't want to be with her. I looked at her pretty, silly face, and I felt suddenly that I didn't like her. It was scary. And at the next table, two men who were having dinner together kept looking over at our table. They weren't looking at Vi. They were looking at me.

Twelve

Nothing was the same. Now Emily was defending Vi, and I was attacking her.

"She's childish and dependent and silly," I said.

"She's very sweet and lighthearted," Emily said.

"Since when are you sticking up for her? You never liked her. You didn't even have to say so. I knew it."

Emily shook her head. "No, Patti, I never disliked Vi. I thought she was very different from my mother. That's certainly true. But I never disliked her."

"Oh, come on, Emily! You made it very obvious how you felt about her."

We were sitting in Emily's room all by ourselves. The room was as messy as ever, and I was grateful for it. So many things had changed since my father's heart attack, I needed to have something that remained the same.

Emily dragged a pillow out from under all the debris on her bed and leaned back on it. "I always thought it was wonderful how close the two of you were. I was just talking to my mother about it the other day, and she said . . ."

"You know, Emily," I said, "I can't keep up. Lately everything is different, and I don't know when it all happened."

"What do you mean?"

"Well, suddenly you're telling me you never disliked my mother, and you keep quoting your mother."

"What's so strange about that? My mother is a psychologist, after all."

"But Emily, you used to hate your mother."

"No," Emily said. "No. I never hated my mother." I started shaking my head, and she said quickly, "Well, she's not like most mothers."

"But—" I began.

"I know." Emily smiled. "I guess I gave her a hard time. I mean, I tried to give her a hard time. I wanted her to be like everybody else's mother . . . like your mother, most of all."

"No," I said. "You shouldn't want her to be like Vi. Vi's not a mother . . . not a real mother."

"I was jealous," Emily said. "Because the two of you always had so much fun together. My mother never had time. Even now, I practically have to make an appointment to see her. But it's okay—now. I don't mind—now. She lets me breathe, so I guess I have to let her breathe too."

The world was changing too quickly for me. "I'm frightened," I told Emily. She reached over and patted my hand.

"Do you want to go with Alex and me to Angel Island on Saturday?" she said. "We're going to take the ferry over and poke around there."

"I'd like to," I said, "but I'd better check it out with Dan."

"Alex likes you," Emily said. "He thinks you're really sweet."

"I'm not sweet," I said. "I don't want to be sweet."

"Yes, you are sweet. You're nice to everybody, and good-natured. You listen to people and kid around. You're sweet, all right."

"I'm not sweet," I yelled. "It's stupid and insipid being sweet. It goes along with being pretty. I don't want to be just pretty and sweet. That's the trouble with Vi. She's pretty and sweet, and I'm not going to be like her."

Suddenly I was bawling again, and that was something new, too. I never used to cry. I never had any reason to cry, or at least I thought I never had any reason to cry. Emily was looking at me in astonishment. "What did I say?" she asked.

But I felt better because it was out there finally—I wasn't going to be like Vi. I wasn't going to be trapped inside of being pretty and sweet and good-natured. I wasn't going to be like Vi.

Before I left, Emily told me that she and her parents were planning to spend five weeks up at their country place in Calaveras that summer.

"We'll go the first week in July. Both my parents can arrange their vacation schedules then. It's beautiful up there. There's a pool close by and also a gorgeous swimming hole in the Stanislaus River, with a real waterfall."

"Sounds great."

"And Alex says he can come up for a week. He already has a job for most of the summer, baby-sitting for a little boy."

"Baby-sitting? Alex baby-sits?"

"What's so strange about that?"

"Well, he's a boy."

"I know very well he's a boy." Emily laughed. "Is there anything wrong with a boy baby-sitting?"

I tried to think of Dan baby-sitting. At first, it seemed hardly possible or even natural for somebody like Dan to baby-sit, but then I realized he must have to look after his little sister, Mollie. So what was strange? So many new things to think about, to sort out in my mind. "No. I guess not."

"Anyway, the family he sits for is taking a vacation around the Fourth of July, and that's why he'll be able to come up that week."

"That's nice," I said stiffly, trying not to show the hurt inside of me.

Emily cocked her head and examined me. "Well, I guess Dan could come up, too, if you wanted to ask him. I'll have to check with my mother, but I think there would be enough room. There are three bedrooms, and a sleeping balcony, and somebody could always sleep on the couch in case my brothers want to come up, too, at that time. No matter how many people come, there's always room. You'll see."

"You mean you want me to come up too?"

"Of course, stupid. I told you I wanted you to come up with me for the whole time."

"No, Emily, you didn't."

"Now, don't start that again, Patti. I know I told you weeks ago and you said yes."

She hadn't. I knew she hadn't. But nothing stayed the same anymore, and nobody saw what anybody else saw or heard what anybody else heard.

On the way home that night, while I was waiting for a light to change, a man asked me "What time is it?"

I looked up at him suspiciously—a tall man with a look in his eyes that I had seen before and that I hated. "Go away!" I told him.

The light changed and I hurried across the street. I felt as if I were being pursued even though there were no footsteps behind me. The whole world was changing around me, and I knew I was going to have to change too. But how?

The door to my parents' bedroom was closed when I entered the apartment, and my grandmother came out of the kitchen and signaled to me not to bang the door.

"He's resting," she told me in a low voice.

"He's had a bad day. I took him over to the hospital, and the doctor changed his medicine." Grandma shook her head. "He had a lot of pain. I could see he was upset, even though he wouldn't admit it."

"What did the doctor say?" I whispered.

"Oh, he said it was going to take time. What does he know?" My grandmother waved her hand angrily and then drew me inside the kitchen. "Nowadays, they're always in a hurry. And your father—he's not a complainer. I told him to tell the doctor exactly what he was feeling, but he just made it sound like a little gas pain."

"Where's Vi?" I asked, looking around the kitchen.

"Oh, her!" my grandmother said in disgust. "I don't know what I'm going to do about her. To tell you the truth, she's giving me the most trouble. Harry is a sick man. He can't really help himself, but he does try to think of other people, but Vi . . ."

"So where is she?"

"Well, she started carrying on when Harry didn't feel well. I could see she was going into one of her tantrums, so I took her into your room, and I told her she'd better cut it out or she'd have a dead man on her hands. Then she started bawling, but quietly at least, and I told her to stay there until we left, and to get herself straightened out before we came back from the hospital. Naturally, I didn't say anything to him."

"So where is she?"

"When we got back, there was this note."

Grandma handed it to me. It was in Vi's handwriting, which I used to copy when I was in the sixth grade—a small and pretty handwriting, with all the *i*'s dotted with little circles. Of course, Vi also used a pen with violet-colored ink. The note said:

Dear Harry,
   I am out shopping and will be home later. Tell Patti I'll take her and Dan over to Tower Records tonight for some new cassettes. They have a sale.
Love and XXXX's,
Vi

"I'm not going," I said.

My grandmother closed the door of the kitchen. "Let's talk," she said. The two of us sat down on either side of the kitchen table and faced each other.

"What are we going to do about her?" I asked.

"Who do you mean?" said my grandmother, narrowing her eyes.

"You know who I mean," I said. "I mean Vi. She's hopeless. She's like a baby—no—not like a baby, because she's a grown woman. She's nearly thirty-two. It's crazy for a woman her age to act so silly and to think of nobody else but herself."

"Now, Patti," my grandmother said. "That's not really true. Vi loves you and she loves Harry, and she's spent her whole life trying to make the two of you happy. It's not right for you to talk about

116

her that way. This is not an easy time for her and—"

"It's not an easy time for any of us," I snapped, "and it sure is funny listening to you defend her. You're the one who's always criticized her the most."

"No, I haven't," said my grandmother, looking surprised. "I haven't criticized her. I love her. She's my daughter, and she's very sweet and . . ."

"Sweet!" I said angrily. "Yes, she is sweet, and that's all she is. She's not responsible. Just look at the way she's fallen apart over Daddy. She's sweet all right, and helpless, and maybe it's your fault she's that way. You're her mother. You should have taught her to behave like a grown-up. You shouldn't have let her get away with acting so silly."

"My fault!" said my grandmother. "My fault!"

"Yes," I shouted. "Your fault."

"Shh!" hissed my grandmother. "You'll wake him up."

"It's your fault," I repeated in a whisper. "You let her get away with being childish and silly. You should have taught her to be responsible, supervised her better, you should have . . ." Suddenly, it was all very clear to me. It was my grandmother's fault that Vi had turned out the way she had.

"Should have! Should have!" My grandmother's face was red with anger. "What do you know about anything? Should have? And who was going to support the family while I was supervising Vi? You spoiled little brat!" My grandmother leaned her face over the table, close to mine. "I was working forty to sixty hours a week in a cleaning store to keep the three of us from starving to death. I didn't have a man who brought home a paycheck every week like your father does. After the divorce, I never got a cent from your grandfather. I never got a cent from him before the divorce either . . . but all right, that's another story. I had to work all week, and then come home and take care of my house and my two kids. Joey was worse than Vi. I had to worry about Joey all the time. He got in with a wild bunch of kids. I was always down at juvy hall trying to keep him out of jail. You didn't know that, did you? But he straightened out, didn't he? And now he's a fireman and he's married, and he'll be all right. Maybe I don't see him much because he lives in Cincinnati, but he's a good boy. He calls me, and he sends me money sometimes. And Vi . . . Vi . . . I didn't want her to have the rotten life I'd had, and she didn't. She was so pretty and sweet. Maybe I should have been stricter with her, but I did the best I could. . . . I never thought she'd get into trouble. And . . . well, you know . . . I hated your father for a while. After all, he was more than twice her age then. He should have known better. She was only a kid, a sweet, innocent kid, and . . . and . . ."

My grandmother's lips were trembling, and I felt ashamed. Nothing was easy. Not even knowing who to blame.

"So maybe I shouldn't have babied her so much," my grandmother went on, "but she did the same with you. She did everything to make you happy. I never said she didn't. Maybe I criticized her for other things, but not for the way she looked after you. So don't go saying she wasn't a good mother. Don't you dare say that about Vi."

My grandmother's fists were clenched, and tears were running down her cheeks. I bent forward, put one of my hands over hers, and whispered, "I'm sorry, Grandma. I'm sorry."

My grandmother took a deep breath, straightened up, pulled a tissue out of her pocket, and jabbed at the tears on her face. I looked away.

"All right now," she said. "Let's calm down and talk."

"Maybe Vi should go back to school," I suggested. "She never finished high school."

"Are you crazy?" my grandmother said. "She always hated school. She never got good marks the way you do."

"I'm not so great," I said. "I get mostly B's."

"B's are good enough," said my grandmother. "Vi never got B's, and she was never interested in school. Why should she be interested now?"

"Well, I thought if she finished high school, maybe she could get a decent job."

"A job!" My grandmother's eyes opened in horror. "What does she need a job for? Your father has plenty of money. Even if he has to stop working because of his heart attack, he'd still have enough. And if, God forbid, anything happens to him, I know he'll leave the two of you more than well provided for. That's one thing about your father—he's always taken good care of his family. I've never criticized him about that."

"Daddy babies Vi too," I said. "She's never worked a day in her life, and it's good for people to work."

My grandmother tapped her forehead with one of her fingers. "Good for people to work," she repeated. "Just listen to her, to the big voice of experience over there." Then she leaned over the table so far her forehead was touching mine. "All my life," said my grandmother, "I had to work at jobs I hated. For twenty-nine years I worked in that cleaning store, and there was never a day I didn't hate it. And before that I worked in a factory making mops, and before that, when I was about your age, washing dishes in a restaurant. God forbid you ever have to work at jobs you hate!" said my grandmother fiercely. "It's not good. No. It's not good for people to work at jobs they hate."

"But if she went back to school and learned something interesting, she could work at something she liked and was good at."

"Like what?"

"Well . . . I can't think of anything off the top of my head, but people have to do something," I said. "Even Vi. Vi has to do something."

"She's been doing plenty," my grandmother said. "She's been looking after her family. She's been taking care of you."

"But now I'm grown up," I said. "You know it, Grandma. I don't need her to take care of me. I don't want her to."

"You're not grown up yet," said my grandmother. "You're only fourteen. You and she are like friends. You were always like friends. Why can't you just go on being like that?"

"No," I said. "No. We're going to have to think of something else for Vi to do. She's not my friend. She's my mother."

Thirteen

Early in May, my father asked me to take a walk with him. It was on a Saturday morning, on one of those days that my grandmother said she wouldn't be able to come, that she had errands to run and affairs of her own to look after.

As always now when she couldn't come, my father fussed and fretted and didn't seem to be able to make himself comfortable.

Vi tried. I had to admit she tried. "How about a movie?" she suggested. "There's a new picture with Clint Eastwood at the Alexandria."

"No!" Daddy said sulkily. "I don't want to go to the movies. And you know I hate Clint Eastwood."

"Well, we can go to another movie then."

"I don't like movies anymore," Daddy said. "They're all full of sex and violence. Not like the movies they used to make."

"I know what," Vi said eagerly, picking up the *TV Guide*. "I think there's going to be a rerun of *Singin' in the Rain* this afternoon. We could watch that, Harry." She looked over at me, almost shyly. "Maybe you'd like to see it too, Patti. Remember how you always used to love it?"

I looked away. Most of the time I tried to avoid seeing that expectant look in her face. She had stopped hanging around waiting for me to come home from school, stopped jumping up and running towards me eagerly as soon as I put one foot inside the door, stopped hoping that the fun was really going to begin once I arrived home. She finally understood that she couldn't count on me any longer to be her pal. Her silly uselessness continued to irritate me, but I didn't feel good seeing how her face emptied when I said no, as I did then.

"I'm meeting Emily later," I told her.

My father was just beginning to say that he didn't want to watch *Singin' in the Rain* when the phone rang. "I'll get it. I'll get it," he cried, hurrying into the hall. We heard him pick it up and begin talking.

"I don't know," Vi said helplessly. "I don't know. . . ."

"Maybe he'd like to go visit somebody," I suggested.

"Who?" Vi asked.

"Well—how about one of his friends?"

"Which friend?"

The panic in her voice irritated me. After all, he was her husband. Couldn't she think of anything to do with him?

My father returned, smiling. "It was Eva," he said. "She'll come for dinner after all. She said she went to the health food store and found a new kind of hot dog. It's made entirely of tofu and doesn't have any polyunsaturated fats or chemicals. Somebody there said it tastes delicious."

Now it was Vi's turn to look sulky.

That's when Daddy asked me to go for a walk with him. "I'll go, Harry," Vi said, making a face. "Patti's busy."

"No, no," I said, feeling guilty. How many times since his heart attack had I taken a walk with him? Generally, it was my grandmother who did. "I'd like to take a walk with you, Daddy. I don't have to meet Emily for another hour or two."

"Good! You don't have to bother, Vi. I know you hate creeping along at my snail's pace. I'll just go for a short walk with Patti, and then later maybe you and I can watch *Singin' in the Rain* together. You just relax. I'll be back soon."

My father's clothes hung on him. Even his hat dropped down too low on his head.

"I'm really getting back into shape," he said, smiling at me out of a face with skin that hung on him just as his clothes did.

"You sure are, Daddy," I said brightly.

"I've lost twenty-five pounds," my father said

proudly. "I'm weighing now what I weighed when I was in my twenties."

"That's wonderful, Daddy!" I could hear him breathing hard as we walked slowly along. "Am I walking too quickly?"

"Well, maybe we could slow down just a little, Patti," he said, leaning on my arm. "Every day, I try to walk a little farther. The doctor says I'm really on my way."

"I know, Daddy. I know."

"Of course, I have to take it slow. I'm not used to living like this, but I know I have no choice. I just have to be patient."

I murmured encouragement as we crept along.

"You girls have been wonderful," my father said, pressing my arm, "just wonderful. And Eva— your grandmother . . ." He wasn't able to finish.

"We just want you to get better, Daddy," I said wearily.

"Let's stop a minute," said my father, leaning against a lamppost, looking pale.

"Are you all right, Daddy?" I asked. "Is something hurting?"

"No, no," my father said, breathlessly. "Let's just stop a moment."

We stood there silently while my father took some shallow breaths. He was not well. He was never really going to be completely well again. I knew it. My grandmother knew it. Perhaps even Vi knew it. I wondered if he knew it too.

"Maybe we can sit down someplace," I said. "How about a cup of coffee?"

"Decaf," my father corrected, smiling. I smiled

back and led him across the street to a small coffee shop.

"You're drinking real coffee, Patti," he said, watching me. "Real black coffee."

"Uh-huh."

"When did you start? You never used to drink coffee."

"Well, I always liked it, but I guess I really started a couple of months ago. They drink a lot of coffee at Emily's house, and I guess I just started doing the same."

"I used to drink a lot of coffee," my father said. He raised his cup and took a careful sip. "It's not really bad, this stuff." He smiled at me. "But it's not the genuine article."

I put my cup down. "Does it bother you, Daddy, if I drink coffee?"

My father shook his head. "No, no, but it just surprises me. I mean, one day you're a baby, and the next you're all grown up." He reached over and patted my hand. "But the way you acted that night I had the attack! That night, I guess you had to grow up fast. I'll never forget it."

"Me neither, Daddy, but thank God it's over."

"Thank God!" he repeated. Then he smiled at me and said, "But there's something I want to talk to you about. That's why I asked you to come for a walk with me."

"What is it?"

"It's about Vi's birthday."

"Vi's birthday?"

"Yes. May twelfth's coming up fast. This year I want to do something really special for her."

I had forgotten Vi's birthday, but as my father went on talking, I tried to look excited and interested as I always had for thirteen of my fourteen and a half years. May twelfth—Vi's birthday, and I had forgotten completely about it.

". . . out to dinner this year, someplace quiet. I know how you girls like to plan superduper parties, but maybe this year we can just go out. Someplace nice, of course, where Vi can eat whatever she likes, and you too, and your grandmother and I can get something healthy. Maybe an Italian place. Pasta's okay, you know. They say now that starches are really good for you. . . ."

I had forgotten Vi's birthday, forgotten all the years of balloons and presents and parties.

". . . not eating cake anymore, but we can order a small one from Fantasia for you and her . . . put up a few balloons. . . ."

Forgotten how especially excited Vi always was over birthdays—mine, Daddy's, or her own. Forgotten how much I, too, had always loved birthdays. Now, suddenly, I was no longer interested.

"What are you getting her?" my father asked. He took another tiny sip and looked at me over the rim of his coffee cup.

"Oh, I don't know. What do you think she'd like?"

"Something expensive," laughed my father. "But you always know best."

"Well, I haven't really thought about it yet, but . . ."

"Poor Vi!" My father put down his cup. "This has been a terrible year for her. Just terrible."

"For all of us," I said quickly. "Especially for you."

He didn't hear me. "I want to make it up to her," he said. "I want her to have a really great birthday. I've got an idea, but first tell me what you're getting her."

"Maybe a scarf," I said. "Or maybe some gloves."

My father put his hand into his pocket and pulled out some money. "Get her something nice," he said. "Something special. I mean from you. Maybe a piece of jewelry or something . . . something special." He handed me four bills— four fifty-dollar bills.

"Daddy," I said, "you know I never spend a lot on Vi. You're the one who does. Not me."

"This year," said my father, "I want all of us to. Even Eva. I told Eva this year it has to be special. I even told her what I want her to get. I'll tell you in a minute about that."

"But Daddy, you should be the one who gets her the special present. I'll shop for you if you want me to. You can get her a pair of earrings or maybe a purse."

"No," said my father. "I've already decided what I'm getting her." He reached over and patted my face. "It's something for you too, Patti. Remember I said I was going to make it up to you?"

"What is it, Daddy?"

My father leaned forward and dropped his voice as if Vi were sitting right near us and could hear what he was going to say. "I'm getting her something she's been dying for ever since we were married—I'm getting her a cruise to Hawaii."

"A cruise to Hawaii! You're going on a cruise to Hawaii with Vi?"

My father laughed out loud. "Of course not. You know I couldn't go now, and even if I could the way I am, she wouldn't have a good time. No, no, Patti, I'm giving her a cruise to Hawaii, and I'm giving you one too. You're part of Vi's birthday present. She'll have you to take with her on the cruise. A real luxury cruise with a top deck cabin—everything the two of you could possibly want."

"Not me," I said. "I'm not going."

He wasn't listening. "Right after school," my father said. "It's for two weeks, and you tour all the islands but sleep on the boat. I told Eva to buy her some luggage, and I'll give you both some money for clothes, and . . ."

"Daddy," I said firmly, "I can't go."

My father swallowed the rest of his sentence and looked at me, puzzled.

"I told you, Daddy, I'm spending five weeks up at Calaveras with Emily and her family. She invited me weeks ago, and I told you."

"Oh, that's right," my father said, shaking his head. "I did forget that, but Patti, you can go to Calaveras any time. Emily and her family will understand that a luxury cruise to Hawaii . . ."

He looked so sure of himself, so positive that I'd rather be going on a yucky cruise to Hawaii with Vi than to Calaveras with my friends, that I almost felt sorry for him as I said, "I'm sorry, Daddy, but I told them I'm going, and I really want to go."

My father straightened up in his chair and looked thoughtful.

"Maybe she and Grandma could go."

"No," said my father.

"Or maybe she could go by herself. It might be nice for her to go by herself. She might make some new friends, and see some new . . ."

"I know," said my father confidently. "You can go when you come back from Calaveras. You can go later in the summer. I'm sure there are other cruises, maybe in August or even September. If you miss a few days of school, that wouldn't be so terrible, would it, Patti?"

"Daddy," I said, very firmly, "I don't want to go on a cruise to Hawaii. I just don't. Not in August. Not in September. Not anytime."

"But why not?" my father demanded.

"Because it isn't something I want to do," I explained. "It's not something kids want to do. It's . . . I just don't want to go. Thanks a lot, Daddy, but I don't want to go."

"But Vi would love to go," my father said. "It's her birthday, and I really want to give her something special."

"Well, like I said, Daddy, maybe she could go by herself or maybe with Grandma."

My father's face tightened. "I never thought you could be so selfish," he said. "After all Vi has done for you, how can you be so selfish? It's just not fair."

Not fair! Inside me a fury erupted at him, at my father, who was sitting there telling me I was selfish and not fair. If his face hadn't been so gray and if I hadn't known how sick he was, I would have stood up and told him that he was the one who had fallen in love with a silly, helpless girl, had married her, and had never let her grow up. It was his fault if Vi had become a burden to him now—his fault. I would have told him that, and I also would have told him that I wasn't going to allow him to sacrifice me just to get Vi off his hands. I would have told him that it wasn't my fault if Vi was unhappy and bored and silly. I would have screamed it all out at him, at my father, sitting there trying to make me feel guilty. I would have told him off. I would have pointed a finger right at him, and I would have yelled, "You! You! You! You are the one to blame."

But he was a sick man. So I took a few deep, deep breaths, and very calmly, very slowly, I persuaded my father to buy Vi a gold ring with a sapphire. I convinced him that she would much rather have a beautiful sapphire ring, maybe with matching earrings, than a cruise to Hawaii.

Fourteen

I never thought about the three of them for most of the time I was away that summer. Most of the time I was too busy thinking about me and re-arranging myself inside a new world that never stopped changing.

"You're different," Dan said when he came up to spend a long weekend in the middle of July. "You've changed."

His face was troubled as he looked at my hair.

"I guess you don't like it this short," I said, smiling, "but I didn't want to have to fuss over it this summer. We go swimming every day. That's why I had it cut this way. I never have to think of it."

Dan licked his upper lip and nodded. "I guess I

like it better long, but Patti, you look okay whatever you do."

"Mrs. Rees says that all men are alike," I told him. "She says all men are basically reactionary about women. If it was up to men, they'd keep all of us veiled, barefoot, pregnant, and long-haired in the kitchen."

I laughed, but Dan shook his head and looked at me, still troubled. We were sitting by the pool in the sun. Neither of us had gone in for a swim yet. Emily and her parents were parked under a tree, in the shade, reading.

"What's that supposed to mean?" Dan asked.

"Well," I explained slowly, "it means that men don't really like women to be liberated. That they're basically old-fashioned, and they want women home, being subservient. Like my father. That's why Vi is so silly."

"That's baloney," Dan said angrily. "And there's nothing wrong with Vi, either."

I shrugged. "So what's been happening in the city?" I said, feeling almost as if I were asking him how things were on the moon.

I could see Dan physically shake away his annoyance before he could answer. "Nothing much."

"Well, what are you doing with yourself?"

Then he began smiling. He looked over at the Reeses, their noses deep in their books, and said in a low voice. "I've been thinking about you." He reached over and took my hand. "I've been missing you."

I gave his hand a little squeeze and said, "I've missed you too."

"Well . . ." he said happily, ". . . well, that's okay then."

"Let's go swimming," I said. "I've really developed my crawl up here. I'll show you."

Dan was a good swimmer. He had even passed his junior lifesaving test, and the two us swam back and forth, back and forth until I tired. Then we clowned around together, picking each other up and climbing on each other's backs until finally, exhausted and shivering, we pulled ourselves out of the pool and flopped down, dripping in the bright sunshine.

My teeth were chattering, and Dan wrapped a towel around my shoulders and let his arm linger there. It felt good. It felt like old times, and for a while, I almost thought it might work out.

"So, Dan," Mrs. Rees asked him that night after dinner as we sat inside in front of the potbellied stove. Mr. Rees was getting a fire going, and Emily was curled up across the room with her nose in a book. Even in the time Alex was up, earlier in the month, Emily had kept right on reading. Alex read too, and most evenings passed with people reading or arguing in front of the stove.

"So, Dan," Mrs. Rees asked, "what have you been doing with yourself this summer?"

"Nothing much," Dan said. "Sometimes I've had to look after my kid sister, Mollie. She's a handful, but she does go to day camp, so most days I'm free until she gets home."

"Does your mother work?" Mrs. Rees inquired politely.

"Yes. She's a nurse. And my father's a cop," Dan added.

"Oh!" Mrs. Rees said with a little surprise in her voice. "That's really interesting. I don't know any cops."

"They're just like anybody else," Dan said angrily.

Emily looked up from her book. She had the ability of being able to read and listen to any conversation that was taking place. "Don't mind my mother, Dan," she said. "She's the biggest snob that ever lived. Just think how lucky you are not to have to put up with it every day."

"Stove is smoking again," Mr. Rees announced, and Dan quickly leaped up and hurried over to help out.

"I'm really sorry, Dan," Mrs. Rees said. "I didn't mean to hurt your feelings."

"I'm sorry too," Dan muttered, not looking at her.

Mrs. Rees turned a contrite face toward me. "I didn't mean anything, Patti," she said. Her eyebrows were lifted slightly, and the next morning, in front of the bathroom mirror, I practiced lifting my eyebrows in the same way, and murmuring, "I didn't mean anything."

"She didn't mean anything," I told Dan that morning after breakfast when the two of us were out walking.

"Oh, yes, she did," Dan said. "She was putting me down. I don't like her."

"It's because you've never met that kind of

woman before," I said. "She's an educated, professional woman with an exceptional intellect."

"My mother is an educated, professional woman too, but she doesn't go around making people feel small and unimportant. Neither does your mother. Mrs. Rees is just showing off—it makes her feel big if she can make somebody else feel small."

"She doesn't make me feel small and unimportant," I told him. "She's been picking out books for me to read—serious books by famous authors like Orwell and Dostoevski. She says I need to stretch my mind. She says I've got a lot of potential, and that I've got to take myself seriously. Mrs. Rees thinks I can do anything I set my mind to."

"I don't like her," Dan repeated.

"Well, I do," I said.

Dan slowed down. "Patti," he said, "I don't know what's wrong, but you've changed."

"I know," I told him, and began walking faster.

He stopped, and tugged at my arm to make me stop too.

"What is it, Patti?" He turned towards me and tried to move us closer together. Both of his hands were on my arms.

"I don't know," I said, stiffening, "but nothing's the same anymore. Everything's different. I want to be different too."

"I'm not different," Dan said. "I'm the same."

"I know," I told him. "Maybe that's what's wrong."

It was a relief after he left. The rest of us settled back into our lazy, comfortable days, swimming and reading in the sun during the day and reading and arguing at night in front of the stove. Nobody thought much about food. Every few days Mr. or Mrs. Rees, along with one or two of us, would go down to the local store and load up the car with supplies—canned soups, spaghetti, packaged breads, cookies, hot dogs, breakfast cereals, popcorn . . . cooking and eating were things to get through quickly.

I sent a few picture postcards home and received one letter from each person in my family. My grandmother's letter said:

Dear Patti,

Thank you for the card. You're lucky to be out of the city. The weather has been horrible—cold and foggy for practically all the time you've been away. We had a leak in the kitchen ceiling the other day because the woman upstairs left her dishwasher on when she went off to work and it overflowed. Some people don't seem to have a brain in their heads.

We are all okay. Your father is talking about doing some work at home. He still thinks he'll be able to go back to the office part-time in a month or so. The doctor says wait and see, but between you and me I'm pretty sure he won't be able to. However, it's good that he's keeping cheerful.

Vi made a new friend—that woman she met in the hospital who had the room next to your father's. But the less said about that the better. I'm the same except that the arthritis in my fingers is bothering me again.

Give my regards to the Reeses, and watch out for poison oak.

Love,
Grandma

My father's letter said:

Dear Patti,

I'm glad you're having such a good time in the country. If you need more money, let me know.

We're all fine. Your grandmother owes me $7,689, because that's how far ahead I am in our gin rummy games. I feel much better. You won't recognize me when you get home. I've lost another five pounds, and really feel much stronger. Some days I can walk nearly all the way to Safeway without feeling winded.

Vi is fine too. She made friends with that young woman, Nancy Jordan, who was in the hospital room next to mine. She is a few years younger than Vi, has been divorced, and has a cute little boy. Vi has been helping her out. It keeps her busy.

Enjoy yourself, and be sure to come back with a beautiful tan. We haven't seen the sun in weeks.

Love and kisses,
Daddy

Vi's letter said:

Dear Patti,

I met Dan in the store yesterday, and he said the two of you had broken up. Too bad! He's really a doll, but I figure you must have met somebody real nice up there. Maybe one of those cute lifeguards? I can't wait to hear all about it when you get back.

Nothing much new here except I have a new girlfriend. Her name is Nancy Jordan, the one who was in the hospital room next to Daddy's. She was having surgery on her knee because she had hurt it ice dancing. She's a real kick. She's twenty-eight, with a darling little boy named Larry. I've been spending a lot of time with her, and it helps make the time pass. Daddy and your grandmother are the same. You're lucky to be away.

Have a wonderful time. I miss you.

Lots of love,
Vi

A few days before going home, I tried to explain to Mrs. Rees how I was feeling. "This has been the best summer I've ever had in my whole life," I told her.

She was hanging a towel over the railing on the deck. It had been another long, lazy, warm, reading day, and we were home now, ready for another long, lazy evening. The rest of us always hung our wet towels on the railing to dry overnight and be ready for the next day. Mrs. Rees' towel never got wet because she never swam. Each day, she wrapped up carefully against the sun, which she never sat in. She wore a straw hat, a loose-fitting tunic that covered her arms, and long pants. At first I wondered why she bothered to take the towel down to the pool, since she never used it, sitting as she did in a deck chair in the shade and never swimming in the pool as the rest of us did. By the end of the five weeks I no longer wondered. Whatever she did seemed right.

"Well, I'm glad, Patti," Mrs. Rees said, straightening out the towel so that there were no folds. She was also extremely neat. Even though I never saw her with an iron in her hands, her clothes always hung on her without a wrinkle. "We've enjoyed having you."

"I think my whole life has changed," I said fervently.

Mrs. Rees looked at me with one eyebrow lifted. Then she said, "Come and sit down, Patti. Over here where we can have some privacy." She led me to a couple of chairs at one end of the deck and motioned for me to sit down next to her. Then she looked at me, waiting. She didn't have to say "What's on your mind?" or "Start talking." Maybe because she was a psychologist, she knew how to get people to talk. Some people, anyway.

"I don't want to go home," I began. "I'm not happy at home."

Mrs. Rees leaned over and straightened the collar of my shirt. "You used to be happy," she said. "Emily always used to tell me how happy you were. What's changed? Is it your father's heart attack?"

"Yes," I said. "That made me see everything else that was wrong."

"Wrong?" she repeated. "What's wrong?"

"Everything," I told her. "But especially my mother."

"What's wrong with your mother?"

"Everything is wrong with my mother." I explained eagerly. It was such a joy having Mrs. Rees all to myself. "Maybe Emily's already told you that she got pregnant at sixteen—with me, I mean. And she had to marry my father. He babies her—he used to baby her, but when he had his heart attack, she couldn't do anything. Now my grandmother comes almost every day to look after him because all Vi wants to do is have fun. All she wants to do is hang out with me and act like she's a kid. It's disgusting."

"Disgusting?" repeated Mrs. Rees.

"Yes," I said. "And now the two of them, my father and grandmother, try to make me feel guilty because Vi has nothing to do. They sit around all day long playing cards and talking about salt-free diets and low-fat diets and cholesterol counts, and they think I should just run around with her and play with her like we're both two silly little teenagers. Like she was when she got pregnant."

"You think they want you to be like her?"

"Yes, I do. But I'm not going to be like her. I'm not going to be silly and empty-headed. I'm going to be different from now on. I'm going to study and read and think. You'll see, Mrs. Rees. I'm going to work hard in school and raise my marks. I'm going to be somebody. Don't you think I'm right? Don't you think a girl should learn to be independent and not let her family force her into being something she isn't?"

"I think," Mrs. Rees said very seriously, "that your family—all of you, maybe your grandmother too, could benefit from some family counseling."

"Counseling," I repeated.

"Yes," she said, drumming with her fingers on the arm of her chair. "You've all been through some great changes, and I think it would help all of you to talk it through with some impartial, professional person."

"Like you?" I said eagerly, knowing that nobody else in my family would be willing to go through counseling. Knowing also that I didn't want to be connected with the rest of them anymore, not even in counseling.

"No, Patti." Mrs. Rees smiled. "I'm not impartial, but I could give you the names of some really good people."

"Could I come and talk to you, Mrs. Rees?" I pleaded. She was getting up now, shuddering slightly as the day turned itself toward evening.

"Of course you can, dear. But, Patti, I'm not always going to be available when you need somebody to talk to. If you decide not to go for professional help, you're going to have to learn how to rely on yourself. Nobody can solve problems for you." There was a note of irritation in her voice. "You should have learned that by now. Nobody—not your mother or your father or your best friend or—your best friend's mother—nobody. Now, let's go inside. I'm freezing."

She patted my arm lightly, and we walked together toward the door. I cried that night when I was by myself. I felt frightened and alone. At first I thought Mrs. Rees had been cruel, and I avoided her the next day. She didn't seem to notice. But the more I thought about it, the more I realized that maybe I was lucky she had not taken me under her wing the way I had wanted. All my life I had been sheltered by Vi, and what I needed now was to find my own way in a world that was scary, complicated, and suddenly very exciting. Mrs. Rees could have been kinder. She could have helped me over this shaky time, but if she hadn't always been there when Emily needed her, why should I have expected her to be there for me? Emily was managing very well on her own. And so would I.

By the end of my vacation, I was talking to Mrs. Rees again, but I had stopped trying to lift my eyebrows the way she did.

Fifteen

I don't stay home much anymore. Neither does Vi.

"You're going out again?" my grandmother says to me.

"I have to go down to the main library," I tell her. "There are some government documents I need to look up."

"But you spent all day at the library yesterday," my grandmother says. "Enough is enough."

Patiently I try to explain that I am doing a report in which I need to correlate statistically the relationship of nutrition to child abuse in different parts of the country, but she waves her hand angrily at me and says, "You're going to strain your eyes. You're going to need glasses if you go on like this."

I laugh and try to tell her that study does not lead to eyestrain, but she's not interested. And even though I don't admit it to her, there are times when I'm studying, particularly when I'm comparing charts with tiny figures, that my eyes do begin to swim. But usually, if I just lean back in my chair and keep my eyes closed until the exploding colors burn themselves out like firecrackers inside my eyelids, I can go on.

How I love those figures—those numbers that add up to something; that lead somewhere. Alex says numbers can be manipulated, that many surveys are weighted and inaccurate, and that I shouldn't be so carried away. But I am. I love the even columns in the charts I work with, and I know now that my future will lie somewhere in the world of figures.

I thought my father would understand. After all, he is an accountant.

"No," he says, "no, I never felt that way."

"But Dad, you must have loved working with numbers if you went into accounting. You must have enjoyed getting everything to work out. Even though I'm not interested in going into accounting, I can see how satisfying it must be. I'll probably get into psychological or sociological surveys. I wish I were smarter. Then I might go into physics, but I know my brain isn't that good."

"Your brain is plenty good," says my father.

"But we—your grandmother and I—we think you're working much too hard in school. I mean, we're happy you're taking school seriously. That's very good, and we hope you'll go on to college. That's very nice. Nowadays, a girl should go on to college but, honey, you need to be having some fun."

"I am having fun," I tell him. "I like studying."

My father reaches out and pats my arms. "Where are all those nice friends you used to have? And how come you're not having any parties? I like it when my girls have parties. You know I'm feeling much better now, and even if I didn't want to hang around here, I could always go over to Eva's. You and Vi always used to plan parties. How come you're not doing it anymore? This is the first year you didn't have a Halloween party, and next week is your birthday. You have to have a party on your birthday."

"No! No!" I say firmly. "No party! I don't want a party. We can go out somewhere for dinner if you like, just the four of us, but I'd just as soon stay home. But no party, Dad! I don't want a party."

"What is it, Patti?" my father asks. "What's wrong?"

"Nothing's wrong," I say carefully, pulling away from him.

"You've changed," he says. "You're so serious— it's not normal. And you don't dress up anymore. I never see you going out with your friends. What's wrong?"

"I have all the friends I want," I say, trying not to show anger. He's a sick man, I have to keep telling myself. "Emily is my friend, and so is Alex, and there are other kids, too, at school, kids you don't know. But Dad . . ." I try again to change the subject, to have an intelligent conversation with him. "Didn't you ever love working with numbers?"

"No," says my father. "I can't say I did. It was something I could do, and my father wanted me to come into the business with him and his brother. But Patti, how about getting yourself some new clothes for your birthday? You always used to love buying new clothes. How about getting yourself some pretty things?" My father reaches into his pocket and begins peeling some bills out of his wallet.

He thinks I'm a freak. So does my grandmother. Neither of them understands that I'm trying to make a place for myself in a world that will be different from theirs.

"Thanks a lot, Dad," I say, as he hands me the money. "I can use it. But not for clothes. I'm saving up for a computer, and I'll just put this money to it."

He looks disappointed. Too bad. He will just have to get used to it, to the new me, not the silly little girl who loved dressing up and going to parties, but the new me. I catch sight of myself in the hall mirror and I frown. My hair is too long, and it curls down around my neck. I need a haircut, but I don't have the time. I am dressed all in dark blue—dark blue parka, turtleneck, jeans. I wish my cheeks weren't glowing such a bright pink. They always turn that way when I'm excited, and my conversation with my father has stirred me up.

I know that people look at my cheeks. Even at the library, working over government documents, I can feel strange eyes exploring my cheeks, and other parts of me as well. "Excuse me," somebody will say, "but can you tell me where the Art and Music Department is?" I tell them, coldly, with no smiles, no giggles, and they go away. They understand that I am seriously working and do not wish to be disturbed.

The No Nonsense Girl, Alex calls me, smiling. But he means it in a complimentary way. Nowadays, I sit with him and Emily down in the lunchroom. Sometimes Mavis Ferber, John Pettis, and Matthew Carpenter join us. They are not the popular kids in school or the student leaders. Mavis is shy, but speaks three languages fluently. John is awkward and a genius. And Matthew is obsessed with computers and probably my pink cheeks. I'm not interested in Matthew, but I do like to talk to him about computers.

Over in the center of the lunchroom is the table reserved for the most popular kids—Dan Green, Ryan Kingman, Joanie Redding, Joey Lee, and Felissa Roth—the group Emily and I used to belong to. I have nothing against any of them, and I hope they feel the same way about me. I talk to them when we meet in the halls or in my classes.

Sometimes I even kid around with them. I like them. They're good kids. And I'm even happy to see Dan walking along the hall with his arm across Joanie Redding's shoulders. He was my boyfriend, and maybe one day when I'm sure who I am and where I'm going, there will be somebody else. But not now.

My grandmother and my father shake their heads and talk in whispers when I'm around. I know they are not satisfied with me, and it's hard to say whether they are more disappointed with me or with Vi.

"You're going out too," my grandmother says to her. She and I are leaving at the same time.

"Yes," Vi says. She holds her head up straight and looks my grandmother right in the eye. She has a new hairdo that has wisps of hair sticking out in different directions, and she is wearing a miniskirt, short black boots, and a black leather jacket. "I'll probably be back late, so you shouldn't wait around, and Harry should go to bed."

"Where are you going?" my grandmother asks, her lips turning downward.

"Oh, I don't know." Vi jangles a chain bracelet on her arm as she reaches up to zip her jacket. "If Nancy wants to go ice dancing, I might just go and watch, or maybe we'll take in a movie." Vi shrugs and moves toward the door. I follow.

"Where's Nancy's little boy tonight?" my grandmother demands.

"With his father," Vi says, stopping to look at

herself in the hall mirror. "He's staying with him the whole weekend, so Nancy won't have to get up early tomorrow morning. That's why I'll probably be late."

"Doesn't she ever stay home with that kid?" my grandmother snaps. "Some mother she is!"

"Bye-bye," Vi says, and then she calls out, "bye-bye, Harry. I'll see you later."

The two of us take the elevator down, and Vi begins laughing. I look over at her with a polite smile. "What's funny?" She has green-colored eye makeup on her eyelids and a strange dark lipstick that looks amazingly good on her. She lost weight over the summer and looks younger and prettier than ever.

"Oh, nothing," she says, looking at me out of guarded eyes.

We get off the elevator, and Vi says, "Do you want a lift, Patti?"

I am about to say no when suddenly I say yes. I don't know why, but I do. "Sure," I say. "Thanks, Vi."

She looks surprised but shrugs and begins laughing again as we walk together to the car. I say, "What is it, Vi? What's so funny?"

She lets me into the car and then goes around to the driver's side, opens the door, and slides in. She doesn't close the door, and in the light of the car I watch her as she keeps laughing and looking at me, appraisingly.

"Okay, Patti, I'll tell you, but promise not to tell them."

"I promise," I say.

"Well." Vi leans closer to me and talks in a low, bubbling voice. "You know how she always tries to answer the phone? You know how she always wants to know who's calling?"

She is my grandmother.

"Uh-huh," I agree.

"Well, lately, Nancy hates to call because if she gets her, she starts right in cross-examining her like 'Where's your little boy tonight?' " Vi can imitate my grandmother and sound almost like her. I laugh, and Vi moves her head back a little to grin at me. Then she wiggles closer and continues. "Well, anyway, Patti, Nancy called today and when she picked it up, Nancy hung up. I don't know where I was. Oh—yes I do. I was getting my hair cut. What do you think of it, Patti?"

I don't say what I really think—that a woman her age shouldn't be dressing up like a teenage punker. "Well," I do say finally, "well, I don't know. It's different."

Vi stretches herself up to look in the car mirror. "I don't know either," she says. "I thought I'd try it once, but maybe it doesn't look good on me."

"So anyway," I say, "then what happened with Nancy?"

"Oh, right. Well, I guess Nancy called again, and again she picked it up. So Nancy hung up again. When I got home, she says to me, 'You know, we're getting a lot of those hang-up calls all of a sudden.' Naturally, because Nancy has to keep hanging up every time she hears her voice.

So she says to me, 'I think it must be some kind of weirdo, and I'm going to get the phone company to put a tap on our phone.' Wait till Nancy hears!"

Vi bursts out laughing, and suddenly I am laughing too. She can't stop and neither can I. She doubles over and buries her face in her hands, and when she finally looks up at me, there are tears in her eyes as there are in mine. I am embarrassed, but I can't stop laughing.

"That's a good one," Vi says, closing the door and starting up the car.

"I really don't know what it is with her," I say, still laughing. "Why does she always have to go running for the phone?"

"Because she's so snoopy," Vi says. "She has to know everything I'm doing and everything you're doing."

"She is a character," I say.

"They both are," Vi agrees. "Did you see that new diet they're going to try? It's got a funny name—Pripikid or Pripikill—something crazy like that. It's got no salt, no fat, no sugar, no meat, no nothing."

Vi starts laughing again so hard the wheel begins shaking.

"Hey, Vi!" I yell but I'm laughing too. "Watch out, Vi!"

She drives me to the library, and on the way she keeps on talking. I listen but I don't say much.

"Nancy's little boy is so cute," Vi says. "He

lisps when he talks, the way you used to. He says, 'I'm a wittle teapot.' I taught him that song. You remember how you used to sing it when you were little?"

I nod but I don't look at her. I pretend to be interested in something outside the window.

"Well, he's going to be three in December, and I'm going to help Nancy plan a party." Vi goes on talking about the party she's going to plan for Nancy's little boy, and all the parties she had ever planned for me flash all at once together through my mind, like a kaleidoscope of cakes and ice cream and presents and bright balloons and pretty candles. Nancy's little boy is lucky, I think suddenly with surprise, to have somebody like Vi in his life.

She is saying something to me now, and I turn to look at her. "Don't mind them, Patti," she is saying. "If you like to study, that's okay. You just go on and study."

She pulls over in front of the library, and I turn to her before getting out. I want to say something and I don't know what.

"You have a good time now, Patti," Vi says softly, and, hesitantly, she bends over and kisses my cheek. Then she looks up at me out of her wide, violet eyes, and I mumble, "You have a good time, too, Vi."

"Thanks, Patti." She straightens up and smiles at me, waiting for me to get out.

"And Vi . . ."

"Yes, Patti?"

"Vi . . . Be careful, Vi."

That's not really what I meant to say. Only I'm not sure what it is.

"Oh, sure, Patti." She laughs, and I get out of the car. I hesitate and look back at her. I want to say something else, but she is looking at her face in the car mirror. So I turn, and hurry up the stairs of the library.